THE LIMOGES DILEMMA

RICHARD WAKE

MANOR AND STATE, LLC

PART I

1

The clutch on the lorry wasn't burned out, not completely, but the smell indicated that it was well on the way. The shifting from a full stop was a series of jerks and revs without much forward motion, until the transmission caught. Luckily, there were almost no full stops after we had stolen it and its two companions from the German depot.

The taking had been laughably simple. The poor kid on guard duty at the gate — the only German on the premises — happened to be taking a leak when we emerged from the nearby woods. Seeing as how the six of us were all wearing German uniforms, he didn't really hurry or seem alarmed when he looked over his shoulder at us as we approached. He was just buttoning up when two of the others grabbed him, one on each arm, while a third began to truss him up with a length of rope he was carrying. Soon the unfortunate sap was hitched to a fence post, about six feet from his piss puddle and eight feet from his precious rifle. All the fake requisitioning paperwork we had planned to use as a bluff remained in my breast pocket, along with the rest.

I argued for killing the unfortunate public pisser. It just

made sense. We had opened the gate and were choosing our lorries. I said, "He saw the three of you. I mean, you were right on top of him."

"He saw helmets and uniforms — he didn't see our faces," Claude said. He was the unofficial spokesman for the group. He also was the one carrying the rope.

"Of course he saw your faces. You were close enough to kiss."

"He was scared to death — he won't remember anything," Claude said.

"Says you. I remember everything when I'm scared to death."

"He won't."

"It's your party. And your funeral."

I drove. Leon picked up the rifle and sat next to me. The rest followed in the other two lorries. We were now a small German convoy about 10 or 15 miles northwest of Limoges, except that we were in the Resistance. Our target, about 10 miles farther west, was a Vichy youth camp. We didn't care about the kids they were busy brainwashing when they weren't using them for cheap labor. What we were after were their supplies: summer clothes and winter clothes, boots, a limited amount of guns and ammunition, canvas for tents, wire for fences, and especially cans of fuel — all the material that was so tough to acquire, especially for a Resistance cell hidden in the nearby mountains. The maquis were never comfortable in whatever abandoned farm or logging camp they happened upon, not for long anyway. These supplies were critical for their survival during the times when their only roof was provided by the branches of the trees.

Leon said, "We should form our own business. We could advertise."

"Krauts for hire," I said.

"Austrian Assassins," he said.

"Austrian Assholes," I said. "Remember?"

"I wish I still had one of those cards," Leon said.

"I wish a lot of things."

We had known each other since we were 17, soldiers in a different war. We returned to Vienna and grew up as an inseparable threesome — Leon, Henry and I. I even had a handful of business cards printed up as a gag — Austrian Assholes, Ltd.; Alex Kovacs, President; Leon Susskind and Henry Fessler, Vice Presidents — and we occasionally slapped them on the table at whatever establishment had over-served us that night, or used them as the punchline of an elaborate mating ritual when we encountered three girls who might be up for a laugh.

It was a long time ago. Now Henry was safe in Switzerland, although the last time we talked, we were no longer talking — if that makes any sense. Leon and I were Resistance fighters who had recently settled in Limoges. On second thought, that sounds a little like we were a married couple where the husband had taken a new job in Limoges and the wife had selected a cute little home with blue shutters. This wasn't that — no wives, no blue shutters, no jobs beyond sabotage and survival.

For this particular mission, our Resistance cell in Limoges, very much a part of the de Gaulle crew, was lending us out to a group of maquisards from the hills because we were native German speakers who could hopefully bluff our way past the guards at the youth camp and scavenge their warehouse. Our job was to get in, get out, and get back to Limoges.

During the planning phase — which consisted of the six of us sitting in the woods for a half-hour, passing around a bottle of Armagnac — they had argued for splitting up Leon and I, so that the first two lorries would each have a German speaker. I took the other side.

"I want Leon with me."

"But splitting you makes more sense."

"Not really," I said. "If they question the second lorry, then they're going to question the third lorry, too — and we're screwed. It's better my way. If they question both of us in the first truck, we'll both be authentic. We have to hope that's enough, and they just wave you two through behind us. Your way, we could be blown from the very start. Better my way."

The others agreed reluctantly because my way was the smarter play. But even if it wasn't, I needed Leon with me. The last couple of months, I couldn't even use the toilet without him holding my hand. There was no way I could get through something like this without him by my side.

Soon enough, we approached the entrance of the camp. The gate was shut, but it didn't appear to be locked. There were two sentries on duty, one of whom raised an arm and showed his palm at our approach. As I slowed the lorry, I reached for the other set of bogus paperwork I was carrying, the requisition forms for the warehouse.

Leon and I, who had spoken French pretty much exclusively for the last few years, actually practiced our German a bit during the ride. After a minute or two of normal conversation, the "practice" devolved into the two of us attempting to one-up each other in a game of vile sexual phrases. Leon won that game. For our entire adult lives, Leon always won that game.

"Halt," the soldier yelled, as I stopped the lorry with a few inches to spare. Then he walked over to my side. The other sentry stayed at the gate.

"What's your business here?" The soldier seemed annoyed at the bother.

"Here are my orders." I handed him the sheaf of papers, six or eight pages, all signed and stamped and containing a bunch of swastikas. They were complete fakes, and if there was a standard requisition form that we didn't know about, we were going to have to begin blasting forthwith. Leon cradled his rifle, appearing as casual as he could manage. But I was sure his eyes were fixed on the soldier, as were mine. We were searching not so much for hesitation in his manner but alarm in his eyes. But I didn't see any.

"This is a lot of shit," he said. "Why at night?"

"Beats the hell out of me," I said.

"This is going to be a lot of fucking work."

"There's six of us — no worries for you fellows."

"But somebody has to check what you're taking."

"Okay," I said. "One of your guys has to sit on a chair with a clipboard and check off what we take. No strain there — he can even keep sucking on his bottle of schnapps while he does it."

"Hah. We never see schnapps here." At which point, I held up a bottle of Armagnac that was sitting on the front seat. Suddenly, the eyes that we continued to study showed some emotion. Well, it was more the entire face, and the emotion it displayed was not alarm, but mischief.

"Okay, I have a better idea," the soldier said.

He walked away and picked up the phone in the sentry post and called inside. In about two minutes, a dozen of the camp kids, roused from bed and wearing only underwear and boots, ran out to meet us. One of them was the leader, although you couldn't tell by his underwear. He was handed the requisition forms, and they all ran to the warehouse. We pulled in the lorries and the camp kids promptly loaded them. The other pretend Germans stayed with their lorries, while Leon and I joined the two sentries in a few very long pulls on the Armagnac bottle and engaged in some typical military conversation. It was then most of all that the game of crude one-upmanship that Leon and I just played became quite useful.

In less than a half-hour, we had three truckloads of supplies and the two sentries had a handful of phony paperwork, the remaining third of a bottle of Armagnac, and the everlasting memory of Leon's description of a gymnastic move performed by a blond he once knew, a blond who was actually a gymnast.

2

The head guy from the maquis wanted us to leave the camp in reverse order, with Leon and I taking up the rear. I didn't like it, seeing as how that way, without any German speakers up front, any encounter with a German patrol would necessarily result in gunfire. The problem, as I had said before, was that it was their party. Also, and not inconsequentially, there was the small matter of me not knowing where we were going, and that there was no map, and that the others couldn't even verbally lay out the route for me. They said they would have to drive it by feel.

"How about this?" I said. "I'll drive in the lead. When you know that a turn is coming up, use your horn — one blast for a left, two blasts for a right. We'll have to take it a little slower, but it should work."

"I don't know." It was Claude, the spokesman. His tone of voice suggested that he felt it was his turn to win an argument.

"It'll work," I said. "You know it will. And it will still leave us with the best chance to talk our way out of trouble if we meet anyone."

Ultimately he agreed, and we were off. Well, we were off

once I got finished stalling the lorry after reversing it away from the warehouse and then straining to get it re-started. Leon snorted when I did it.

"The hell with you — I did it on purpose," I said.

"Right."

"No, really. Our buddy in the next truck is a little embarrassed that he's lost a couple of debates with me. So this way, he can make fun of my driving and save face with the others. Everybody's happy."

"Always thinking, always in control," Leon said. Then he smiled — something neither of us had done much in recent times.

"What's so funny?"

"Nothing," he said. "It's just nice to see the old you is still in there, somewhere."

For the next five minutes or so, neither of us said anything. I don't know what I was thinking about, but it was disrupted by two quick blasts on the horn coming from behind me. I made the next right turn, and the other two lorries followed. The signal had worked, at least the first time. We were headed up into the mountains.

"Okay, this is going to work — hand me that other bottle," I said.

The cognac was rolling around under Leon's seat. He uncorked it and passed it my way. I took a long drink, and when he held out his hand I ignored him. Then I took a second drink. The sensation was somewhere between warming and burning inside me, probably closer to burning. Leon snatched the bottle from my hand without asking.

"Just fucking drive," he said.

"Yes, Mother," I said.

We were headed to an abandoned chateau. That was all I knew. When I heard chateau, my mind tended to run toward powdered wigs and harpsichord music and bowing servants and unmatched views of the valley below, a legion of serfs bringing in the crops as entertainment. It was probably just an old dump, but whatever. You can't control your imagination.

After his admonition, Leon waited a healthy two minutes before taking a drink out of the bottle himself. Then he said, "How long have we been here?"

"What do you mean by here? France? Earth?"

"Limoges, asshole."

"Six weeks."

"Seems like longer somehow."

"Not to me," I said. And then we were quiet again.

Six weeks earlier, Leon and I had been smuggled out of a safe house in Lyon, first into a lorry and then into a railroad freight car, hidden behind large wooden cases stacked nearly to the ceiling. We were there after an airplane extraction that was supposed to take me and my wife Manon to England was botched. I was shot but all right to travel pretty quickly. And so it was Leon and I, plus a Jewish family — a widower and his two teenage sons, 16 and 14. Limoges was the destination where we would stay and the Jews would be ferried toward Spain.

It wasn't a very big space, so we all became quite intimate. It turns out that taking a shit in a bucket 10 feet away from a couple of strangers tends to remove a lot of the superficial social barriers rather quickly. As was common with people our age, one of the first topics of conversation was what we did in the Great War. Leon took the lead. I really didn't have much to say.

We saw plenty of shit in our war, but Leon and I also had some fun. At Caporetto, we not only won the big battle, but we also got to chase the Italians down the mountain, stopping at some of the nicer houses along the way and relieving them of whatever happened to be stored in their wine cellars. Leon owned a well-worn roster of tales — wine, women, all of that.

Jacob, the widower, was not as lucky. He was at Verdun. There were no raided wine cellars at Verdun. "Even the whores they brought in for us were ghosts," Jacob said. The eyes of the two boys widened beyond all human ability at that point. Then Leon told one of his go-to stories, in which a mother, a skinny daughter and a fat daughter all played a part, and I thought the two boys were going to pass out.

Later that night, with the boys asleep, Leon leaned over to Jacob and said, "Sorry about the stories in front of the boys. I just got carried away."

"Don't even think about it," Jacob said. "I'm so glad you told them. You have to realize, the worst day of their lives was when their mother died. Nothing can change that, nor should it. These days right now should be the next worst. But now, thanks to you, they won't be. They'll always talk about you, Leon."

"And the fat sister," I said.

I had barely participated in the conversation. I had barely said anything for two-and-a-half days, other than to excuse myself as I squeezed past everyone to use the bucket.

Jacob pointed to my hand, at the wedding ring.

"You're married," he said. Not a question.

"Yes." I barely got the word out.

"Where is your wife?"

"I don't know," I said.

That was what was in my head as we drove in the mountains, through a couple of miles of trees and then a small town. It was like a million other French small towns. It was one street long, and all the buildings were on the same side. There was a combination city hall and post office. There was a general merchandise store, a bakery, a butcher and a place for fruits and vegetables. There was a cafe at one end of the street and a bar at the other end, the kind with a zinc-topped counter where, in normal times, you could stand and have a coffee in the morning and something fortified in the evening. These being less than normal times, though, it was likely as not to be ersatz coffee in the morning and nothing at night, unless the proprietor had been able to work some black-market magic.

Of course, this late at night, the whole town was dark as we rumbled through — three trucks in a row, with Leon and I in the first one... Leon and I and my memories.

The road bent hard to the right after we passed the bar. It was there that I saw the headlights that suddenly blinded me, and the German soldier waving at me to stop.

3

There were two of them, each of them armed. We had four rifles among the six of us. I was worried, but I wasn't worried, as long as it was just the two of them.

I should have had a third set of fake orders, just for this happenstance. If whoever was in charge of planning the operation had spent more than a half-hour on the task, they would have thought of it, too. But they didn't, and now I didn't have anything other than my wits. My drinking had probably dulled those just a bit, but it had also likely boosted my gumption. This was really going to be fine. I believed that even as I watched Leon begin to finger the trigger on this rifle.

"Where are you headed so late?" It was the Bosch at my side window. He was unarmed. His partner at the passenger-side window was carrying his rifle by the sling on his shoulder. No worries. No worries.

"A new youth camp." In the 20 seconds or so between seeing the headlights and the conversation beginning, I decided upon a tale that tracked the truth, sort of. The one worthwhile piece of paper I had in my pocket was a receipt that the sentry at the camp had signed. Even if he hadn't signed it, even if we'd had to shoot everyone there to get what we needed, I would have scrawled something on the signature line, along with the date and time.

"Don't ask me why, but we're moving all of this shit from that camp into a new camp up these fucking hills." I handed him the receipt and allowed him to puzzle over it for a while. Then I snatched it back

"I need it for my boss," I said. "It'll be my hide if I don't have it."

"Where is this new camp?" The soldier seemed skeptical. He also had identified my weak spot, seeing as how I had no idea where I was.

"This is where I can get in trouble," I whispered, almost conspiratorial. I was also half-smiling an I'm-an-idiot smile, which came naturally to me.

"I lost the map," I said. "But I looked it over earlier in the day. I don't know where it is — probably wedged in with the paperwork I had to leave at the last stop. But my memory says I make this right here." I pointed to the right of his vehicle. "And then, in between five and 10 miles, I make another right at a decent-sized crossroads. Then I just drive until I hit it."

"I don't know, not much up that way except goats." The soldier still wasn't buying it. He thought for a second before saying, "You've got no orders. You've got no map. You've got shit, as far as I'm concerned — and aren't you a little old to be a sergeant? Get out."

"You've got to be kidding me. We're late already."

"Out." He wasn't kidding. Neither was his pal, who had slipped the rifle off his shoulder. He was beginning to raise it to point it at Leon when the shot pierced the night. It also pierced the soldier's shoulder, and he dropped the rifle as he fell. Meanwhile, the guy on my side panicked when he realized his weapon was 20 feet away in his vehicle. Leon was already pointing his rifle at him and I said, barely above a whisper, "Okay, don't move."

Soon, all of us were on the road, surveying the situation. The shot had come from the lorry behind us, from Claude. He was a good shot — I could give him that.

"Was that really necessary?" Leon said.

"Yeah, I thought so," he said. "But I didn't kill him. He'll live."

"We'd better hope none of his friends are nearby."

"All the more reason to get moving."

"We should kill them both," I said.

"What's with you?" Leon said. "Stop talking like that."

"They saw us."

"So? We're nobodies."

"I'd like to keep it that way."

"We're not even going to be here—" Leon said.

"It's a goddamn war and they're goddamn soldiers," I said. "What is the problem here?"

"Forget it," Claude said. "Fewer German bodies, fewer French reprisals." Then he ignored me and took control, telling the guy who had been driving him to take the soldiers' vehicle, drive it into the woods and douse the lights, then telling the men from the third lorry to tie up our new friends with some of the wire we had snatched from the youth camp. The whole thing didn't take five minutes.

"We're going to lead now," the spokesman said, looking directly at me. "You're in the rear. Understand?"

"It's your party," I said. During the five minutes, I had grabbed the bottle of cognac from our lorry and had a couple of drinks. Leon took it from me and walked around to the passenger side. The others got to their lorries and began pulling ahead.

I walked over to the two wire-bound Germans. They were sitting up against a wooden fence, one of them moaning quietly from the gunshot wound, and the other looking more defiant than scared. With the bottom of my boot and one mighty thrust, I wiped the defiance off his face. His nose exploded. I did my best to scrape the blood and snot off the bottom of my boot and onto the dirt of the road before getting back into the lorry. But I really didn't care that much either way.

4

The cafe was on the Place de Bancs. Funny name, that, seeing as how there was only one bank. But there were two pharmacies. I guess there wasn't enough nobility or stature in the name Place de Pharmacies, though. So Place de Bancs it was, a promenade that led into the warren of streets and alleys that made up the oldest infrastructure of Limoges.

There were a dozen tables on the wide sidewalk outside the cafe. The mid-afternoon sun was warm. Three of the tables were occupied by me and two others, all single men. At 43, I was junior to the others by at least two decades. They were nursing their drinks. I was not.

I closed my eyes. I had sat in this spot enough times over the last few weeks that I could picture the businesses without seeing them. They were all on the ground floor of five-story buildings, with apartments stacked above. Left to right: pharmacy, bank, barber, pharmacy, tabac, boulangerie, women's clothing store. I didn't need to open my eyes to see that they were all some variation on the concept of empty, even the barber. Because even though rationing did not affect the rate of hair growth, every spare centime was headed for the black market to purchase something as prosaic as a pear or something as practical as a cognac. One of the old men sharing the sidewalk with me looked as if he had cut his hair with hedge clippers but his glass was full. Choices.

I had taken care of all my daily business on this street. My first stop was the bank for a withdrawal. I had made and inherited a good amount of money before the war, and it was spread across some of Europe's finer financial institutions. Some was still in Vienna, presumably. Some was in Zurich, and I was sure that was safe, guarded by those Swiss thieves with the same vigor that they guarded their own money — as long as they continued to get their percentage. Some was in Lyon, but there was really no way to get at it, not given how I left.

The rest had been in Paris, in an arrangement that had pre-dated the war. When Leon and I arrived in Limoges, we took a chance by walking into the bank down the street and arranging for a transfer of some of those Paris funds. The risk was that the Gestapo had already circulated my name as far as Paris — Alex Kovacs, wanted for the attempted murder of a Gestapo officer in Lyons, armed and dangerous, blah, blah, blah — and this would create a trail to Limoges, but it wasn't that big of a risk. Besides, it wasn't that much money because we weren't staying long.

My second and only other stop of the day was the cafe. My diary was a tad light those days. If you had cash, you could have real coffee, a ham sandwich and cognac — all without having to worry about any pesky ration tickets. You had to eat inside, to avoid any undue attention, but you could take your libations out in the sun. I was about four deep when Leon arrived, again with the disapproving face.

"Christ, it's not even 3 o'clock," he said.

"And what do you know of Christ, exactly?" Leon was Jewish, after all.

"I swear like a Frenchman now. It's part of the cover."

"So are you going to sit there and preach at me or are you going to have one?"

Leon decided to have one. It really would have been rather glorious — the alcohol softening the edges, the warm autumn sun — if not for the occasional rumble of a German military vehicle on the cobblestones, breaking the silence. If not for that, and for the intrusion of memory.

"So while you've been lubricating, I've been working," Leon said.

"Working? In a factory? Making porcelain? Bowls? Vases?"

"Shut up. I went to see our friends."

"Same place?"

"Yeah," Leon said. "But they're moving, I think tomorrow. It's been over a week."

When Leon referred to "our friends," he was talking about our Resistance contacts. We were beholden to them for at least a little while longer, Leon said — they had taken us in, after all, after the train arrived from Lyon. At one point, just to be an asshole, I asked Leon where it was written down that we owed these people anything.

"We run risks, they run risks, why do we owe them anything?"

"Because it's just right," Leon said.

"What's right got to do with anything in France in 1943?"

"Come on, they fucking saved our lives."

"And we saved other lives," I said. "We didn't ask for payment. We just did it. We don't owe these people anything."

"A couple more weeks. Besides, I still need to figure a way to get us to Paris," Leon said. His voice was quieter now. I didn't say anything. The waiter came outside and re-filled my glass without asking. He looked at Leon and received a nod in reply.

"So how are our buddies in the TAR?" I asked. That was my

abbreviation, for the benefit of Leon and no one else. TAR: Tight-Assed Resistance.

"They're not so bad."

"But you've never told me: do you think they only kiss their pictures of de Gaulle before they turn out the lights at night, or do they actually jerk off while looking deep into his eyes?"

Leon laughed at that one. "Nothing so crude. But I do think they like to keep the pictures in this pocket," he said. He patted the left side of his chest. "You know, close to their hearts."

When I asked about the "same place," I meant the Cour du Temple, really a beautiful, tranquil spot that wasn't a five-minute walk from where we were sitting. It was a few centuries old, a courtyard of half-timbered buildings and urban solitude. On the third floor of a hotel that formed one part of the frame of the courtyard, in Room 311, our de Gaulle-loving contact was running the operation. His radio guy lived in a flat a few streets over. His couriers were mostly kids — the oldest was probably 16 — scattered all over the neighborhood, often unbeknownst to their Vichy-loving parents. It was in Room 311 where we were given our instructions to meet up with the maquis and the basics of the youth camp scheme.

"Did the asshole ever say 'thank you,' by the way?"

"Not in so many words," Leon said. I didn't attend the debriefing after we returned. The less time I spent with those people, the better. On that, Leon and I agreed.

"Good job? Appreciate it? Nice work?"

Leon was silent, and just sipped his drink.

"But we still owe them?"

"Just a little longer," he said. He stood up. "I have to go now — I'm making a little delivery for them."

"Of course you are."

"It's nothing."

"If it's nothing, let one of those kids do it."

"There's no risk."

A German truck rumbled past. Two uniforms eyed us up as they drove by, but they never slowed.

"And if those two decided to get out for a chat?" I said. "And if they asked you to empty your pockets? What would they find?"

"Two identity cards — a Jewish husband and wife. They're both about 25. We can get them out of here. They can still have a life."

I didn't say anything. Leon thanked me for the drink and walked away. I alternated between dozing and opening my eyes whenever I heard footsteps that might belong to a woman — seeing if she might be the same size, the same age, with the same hair.

5

It was about 10 o'clock the next morning and the sun was warm and wondrous on my face. If not for the punishing hangover — other than Leon, it was my most loyal friend — I might have felt human, standing there in my undershirt, my face unwashed, my hair wild.

I was standing outside the bar where Leon and I had taken a pair of upstairs rooms. It was a couple of blocks from the cafe on the Place de Bancs and quite convenient. As Leon said, "Two minutes' walking time, four minutes' stumbling." He was well aware that I was on the four-minute plan pretty much every night.

The bar was owned by a guy named Louis. He had some Resistance ties, I think through marriage somehow, but the ties were loose and reluctant. Leon and I were sent here by the de Gaulle worshippers when we arrived in town, and Louis agreed to rent us the two rooms directly above the bar; Louis and his wife and son lived in a proper flat on the floor above that. But there was a condition.

"No meetings here," Louis said. "No planning. No nothing. You sleep here, you shit here, and that's it."

The rent was a pittance, mostly because the rooms were full of bar stink and the bathroom was, well, interesting — you know, in the manner of a school science project. I made a counteroffer: I would pay double if Louis gave the bathroom a proper scrub and if he allowed us to drink for free.

"What's proper?"

"Clean enough for your wife to sit on the seat."

"Five drinks a day or 100 drinks a month," is how Louis countered my counter.

"Deal," I said, secure in the knowledge that I would be able to sneak an eye-opener or two most mornings without it counting against the total.

I ran my tongue across my front teeth and tasted the remnants of that eye-opener. Leon was out already, a man with a purpose. The neighborhood, once the bastion of the butchers of Limoges but now more of a mixed lot of merchants and residents, was beginning to wake up. Stores were opening, even the ones with no hope of a single transaction. The women were starting their daily trek to try to find something to cook for the family dinner, ready to spend hours in waiting lines for whatever happened to be available. And I was standing there in my undershirt, unwashed, unshaved, alone.

About 10 steps behind me as I looked out on Rue du Canal was the Chapel of Saint Aurelian. It was supposedly built in the 1500s, but it looked even older than that. It was a tiny pile of stone — I bet it wasn't 20 feet wide. I had seen it every day since we moved in. There was no way to avoid it. It was so close to the bar that the less ecclesiastical patrons who drank outside on warm nights occasionally pissed against the chapel wall rather than using the facilities inside the bar.

I don't know why I chose to go inside the chapel, seeing as how I had always counted myself among the less ecclesiastical. There were about 20 wooden chairs for congregants, with an elaborate altar beyond, all old and dark and cold. It was really a creepy little place, and I don't know why, but I just closed my eyes and began crying.

Three years earlier, Manon and I had been married. I had never been able to commit, not for my whole life, but with her I knew that it was right and that it would be forever. Our life together in Lyon was a constant terror, me on sabotage missions and she writing and distributing a small Resistance newspaper, but that terror just seemed to heighten our feelings for each other. And then, with the news of Manon's pregnancy it was as if — even amid the Nazi hell — the life I had always wanted was going to be mine. When the Resistance agreed to fly us to England after a particularly dangerous mission left us as prime Gestapo targets, I actually allowed myself to dream a little.

Even when the thing was botched, and I was shot and left in France, at least Manon had appeared to get to the plane, and the plane had taken off.

But then the plane was never heard from.

We had sat before the radio in the safe house where they were hiding us, night after night after night, waiting for some kind of message that Manon's plane had gotten through. We listened to the BBC's broadcasts, to the personal messages, for any news, for just a hint. But there was none. The plane had not made it back to England. That much, we were sure of.

But there were a couple hundred miles of northern France between Lyon and the Channel. Could it have been shot down, or crashed someplace? As the days and weeks passed, my hopes shriveled to about nothing. The Resistance was everywhere in northern France, loosely organized in some cases but organized nonetheless — and really ubiquitous, much more than in the south. The word was put out, for any word on a small plane crash, for any sightings, for any survivors. Nothing came back in reply. They want so far as to jeopardize future operations by asking questions of Resistance cells in specific areas that tracked the typical flight pattern for such secret air missions in the Lyon area. But no one saw anything.

In the midst of a war, in a world where every human emotion and experience seemed to be accelerated by events, my grieving was shockingly short. I concluded pretty quickly that Manon and our unborn child were gone forever, likely into the Channel, maybe shot down by a German battery along the coast, maybe just a mechanical mishap. The grief had morphed and, most days, it was only the anger that lingered. There was work to be done, after all, the work of surviving most of all. It wasn't long before Leon and I were secreted behind the cargo in that freight car headed for Limoges.

So mostly it was anger, and even that was tempered by the alcohol into a kind of emotional exhaustion. Usually, I didn't feel anything other than tired. But this day was different. When I opened my eyes and stared at the altar, I could feel my lip quivering and the tears on my cheeks. I actually heard myself calling out, "Why me?" It was like a scene in a bad movie, but it was how I felt. Why me?

I was sobbing. My whole body was shaking. I actually said out loud, in the middle of a holy place, "Why? Why the fuck why?"

I got up and knocked over the chair I had been sitting on. The clatter echoed in the stone chapel, and I left the chair laying on its side. I opened the door and a shaft of the morning sun lit up the cold, dark sanctuary. Then I closed the door just as quickly as I had opened it — quickly and hopefully silently, considering the Gestapo car parked right outside and the man in the black trench coat pounding on the bar's door.

6

I had no idea if the Gestapo man had seen the door. If he had, I figured he would be over within a few seconds. The only handy weapon was one of the frail wooden chairs. It wouldn't kill him if I hit him over the head with it. It might not even knock him out. But it might stun him for a few seconds, enough time for me to scoot through the door and into the streets.

I stood to the side of the door with the chair held over my head, ready to slam it down on the first person that entered. But 30 seconds turned into a minute, and then into two minutes, and the door never opened. I figured I was okay. Well, maybe.

I looked around. There were a couple of bronze statues up on the altar, off to the sides. Saint Some-such, presumably. The chapel was dark enough, and the statues were big enough, and there also was a chair to the side of the altar. If I moved the chair a couple of feet, and ducked behind it so I'd be hidden by one of the statues, I wouldn't survive a thorough search but I would survive a quick peek. So that's what I did.

How long to wait? I couldn't hear anything outside, not through the thick stone walls. Also, I didn't have my watch, so I could only guess at the time. I always carried my money with me but not the watch because it annoyed me while I slept. But I figured I had to give it at least 15 minutes, which would give the Gestapo man enough time to rouse Louis, ask him a few questions and search the rooms. The search wouldn't take two minutes, honestly. Both rooms were furnished with a bed and a night table. Leon and I each had one spare set of clothes in a knapsack, and that was it. There wasn't anything to find.

Fifteen minutes. I didn't know what to do, so I just counted to a thousand, giving myself some leeway. Concentrating on the numbers helped to calm me down some. My nerves left me in desperate need of relief, but even someone of my ecclesiastical standing was not going to piss inside the chapel. So between my bladder and the counting, there was enough to take my mind off of the fact that I might be seconds away from arrest.

998, 999, 1000.

I crept out from my little hiding place and toward the door. It swung outward. That helped me because even a small opening would give me a clear look at the Gestapo car. If the swing had been inward, I would have had to open it wide enough to poke my head out and look to the left. So I did my best to move the door only an inch, only enough for me to take the smallest of peeks. I hadn't noticed the last time if the hinges would scream or squeak — either would potentially give me away. But they were silent as the door opened. Maybe the noise would come after the first inch.

Then I saw: the courtyard outside the chapel was empty, save for the stack of tables and chairs outside the bar. Louis was outside, hosing them down, just like any other morning.

"Who were they looking for?" I said.

"Not here. Inside."

He turned off the water and re-wound the hose, and we went

into the bar. Louis poured us each a drink. We silently toasted nothing and slugged it down. He poured another.

"So who were they looking for?"

"You."

"Not Leon?"

"Just you," Louis said.

Just me. That didn't make a lot of sense to me. Leon and I had been together more than apart since we'd arrived in Limoges, but he had been the one to spend more time with the Gaullists and he was the one who ran the occasional bit of courier work on their behalf while I was getting shitfaced. If anyone had run more risks and been more exposed, it was him.

"What name did they ask for?" Louis reached into his pocket for a scrap of paper.

"I wrote it down," he said. "Alex Kovacs. That's the name they asked for. Is that you? I thought your name was, what, I forget. Kampe?"

"Alex Kovacs is one of my names, but I didn't tell you that," I said, not bothering to tell him that it was my real name. Louis was in deeper than I ever expected.

The fact that they were searching for my real name left me with two possibilities. One was that the Gestapo in Lyon had managed to track me to Limoges, because they knew my real name despite the succession of aliases and fake identification cards I had obtained in the previous couple of years, including Albert Kampe. They knew my real name because the officer I tried to kill, Werner Vogl, had known my real name before the war. If they had tracked me from Lyon to Limoges, that meant the entire operation in Lyon had been compromised. It was possible — anybody would talk when they started lopping off your fingers with a rusty knife — but I didn't think so, though I still found myself reflexively counting my fingers in silence.

That left the other possibility: the bank transfer from Paris.

That seemed more likely because of the paper trail the transfer had created. At the same time, though, it wasn't a ton of money, not a sum that would raise a Nazi accountant's eyebrow. So did they have my name on some kind of master list, and that somehow raised the alarm in some back office in the First Arrondissement?

The difference between the two scenarios potentially mattered. If Lyon was after me, and caught me, I was as good as dead. But if it was about the money transfer, it might just be a routine inquiry. When the Gestapo was involved, even the routine was frightening, but maybe that's all it was.

None of this mattered to Louis, though.

"You have to get out," he said.

"I know."

"Both you and the other guy."

"I know."

"With my family, I just can't."

"I know, Louis. I know."

I went upstairs and packed my shit, and then Leon's. It didn't take a minute because we really didn't have anything. Our current lives now fit into two small knapsacks, not much bigger than the ones a worker would carry his lunch in, back when people brought a decent-sized lunch to work with them, before the rationing. I was just glad that I had withdrawn almost all of the money from the account on Place de Bancs the day before, as there was no way I could chance another visit.

I brought the knapsacks down to the bar and sat in the same place. There was another drink waiting for me.

"I have my stuff and Leon's, too."

"What if he comes back?"

"Tell him what happened, and that I have his knapsack at the TAR. Can you remember that? TAR."

"What is that, some kind of code?" Louis wrote it down on

the same scrap of paper where he had written my name. He looked nervous. I was going to say something to calm him, that TAR wasn't any kind of dangerous code, and then he blurted out what was really on his mind.

"You know, there's no refund," Louis said.

"I kind of figured," I said. "So at least give me a chance to drink my way close to even. It shouldn't take an hour."

7

As I walked over to the Cour du Temple, I remembered through the alcoholic haze what Leon had told me the day before: that the Resistance was getting set to move. I thought he said they were moving that day, and I had no idea where. This would be a reasonably significant problem, seeing as how I didn't have anywhere else to wait for Leon.

I walked into the small alley that soon opened onto the charming courtyard. It really was a peaceful spot, a feeling that I enjoyed for at least five seconds. Then it was into the hotel door on the right and up the stairs to the third floor. Room 311 had been the headquarters, and that is where I knocked the secret knock — three knocks, wait a second, then two knocks. The door opened, and I was admitted to the chaos, with three men packing the operation into three small suitcases. It wasn't much — some Resistance pamphlets, the precious carbons that would be used on a Roneo duplicating machine, blank paper and stamps used for counterfeiting ration tickets, that kind of thing.

"Where's the Roneo?" I asked the one face I recognized, another Louis. This was an occupational hazard if you were involved with French Resistance fighters. Everybody wanted to be Louis, for some reason — and that didn't include the people who really were named Louis.

"It's in pieces in those two," he said, pointing at two larger suitcases.

"That's impressive. How long to put it back together?"

"Not that long, especially if you're not too fussy about having a leftover part or two when you're finished," he said.

They were almost done. One of the last things thrown into the last bag was the picture of de Gaulle on the desk. It was in a gold frame.

"Seriously?" I said. "Is your mother's picture in that nice a frame?"

"My mother supports the Vichy," Louis said.

"Must make for interesting dinner conversation."

"It did until it didn't. I haven't been home in almost a year."

"Sorry about that," I said, and I meant it, his de Gaulle fetish notwithstanding. Hell, he probably wasn't even 25 years old — and Limoges was a bit of an odd place. They all talked about their great Resistance tradition, but the city was crawling with Vichy lovers. The Resistance fighters might have been brave and true and all of that, but they were a tiny minority. At least it seemed that way.

"What are you doing here, by the way?" Louis said.

I told him what had happened at the bar, about the Gestapo man and the search. He stopped my story in the middle, then motioned. The first guy had left with two of the suitcases soon after I walked into the room. The motion was for the second guy to leave with two more suitcases, leaving Louis, the final small satchel, and me in Room 311.

"So they didn't ask about Leon?"

"No, just me," I said.

"Good. Good. You have any theories?"

I told him about my two possibilities. He just nodded along, not offering an opinion about which he thought was more likely. Honestly, I was having a little trouble getting past the "Good. Good." It was odd, given our pre-war lives when Leon was the rebel and I was the do-gooder, that as far as these guys were concerned, I was the asshole in this situation. Louis didn't seem to care if I got caught or not, as long as Leon was still clean. At least, that's the way I read it. Then again, I had been drinking, which if it wasn't already apparent to Louis, immediately became so after I belched out a stomach full of alcoholic fumes into the small room.

"A little early, no? Jesus, what time is it?" he said.

"Time to find me and Leon a new place to stay."

He rattled off an address from memory. "Third floor, top of the stairs, the door will be unlocked. Go there now. Leon will meet you there, eventually."

"What do you mean, eventually?"

"After he contacts us, we'll tell him."

"Does he know where you're going?"

"He does."

"Well, where is it?" I asked.

"You have no need to know."

"What do you mean? What's this bullshit?"

"It's not bullshit," Louis said. "It's just smart operationally. You know how this works: small cells of people, one cell doesn't know the other, information compartmentalized, need-to-know. And you don't need to know where we're going."

"So what happens after that?"

"Give us a chance to think, Alex. I can check with my people, maybe with the Brits. We'll come up with something. We might get you out of town for a bit. There's a Commission meeting in Saint-Junien. I was thinking of having Leon represent us this time. Maybe you can go with him."

The Commission was the informal consortium of Resistance

groups in the region who were all supposed to be working together and with the British operations people. As best I could tell, and from what Leon had gathered, these guys and the Brits were quite comfortable in each other's pockets, and they only told the Communist Resistance groups what was absolutely necessary for coordination purposes. An educated guess was that the Communists were just as wary, cooperating only because it was their sole way to get a share of the British weapons and money that were being parachuted into the region. I honestly believed that all of these people spent half of their time thinking about fighting the Germans and the other half maneuvering for a potential power grab once the Germans were gone.

"I'll only go to the meeting on one condition," I said.

"What's that?"

"That I get to be the one who brings the de Gaulle picture in the gold frame."

Louis laughed, a little. "We tend not to bring that to the meetings," he said. "And one more thing: go fuck yourself."

He picked up his little satchel and walked out. I gave him two minutes and then followed behind.

8

The safe house indeed seemed safe — third floor, top of the stairs, door unlocked, dead quiet. I locked myself in, lay down on the bed and was asleep almost immediately. The falling adrenaline and elevated alcohol levels in my bloodstream combined to be a quite effective sedative, as it turned out. It was four hours later when the knocking on the door woke me up. It was Leon.

I went through the events of the morning with him, as I had with Louis. He had a definite opinion about why the Gestapo was knocking.

"It's the money," he said. "It's the bank account. It's an account registered to a Czech who was living in Vienna when it was opened, which means you're a person who should be under the Germans' thumb—"

"As should you," I said.

"But I don't have a centime to my name, as you well know. No, it was the money. Think about it: if they thought they had a lead on the guy who tried to take out the almighty Captain Werner Vogl in Lyon, they would have tried a little harder at the bar than a couple of questions and a cursory search. I'm sure of it. It's the money. They just want to know why Herr Alex Kovacs of Vienna is in Limoges all of a sudden. It's official curiosity. That's it."

"But if they do the least bit of cross-referencing — and these pricks are the kings of cross-referencing, as you well know — they'll find out about Lyon—"

"Among other things—"

"Exactly, among other things. This might just be the beginning."

"Which is why we have to keep moving," Leon said.

"But where?"

"Here tonight, and then they gave me a list of places."

"On paper?"

"No, up here," Leon said. He jabbed at his temple with his right index finger. "I have four addresses memorized. They suggest two nights in each place and no more. When we get through the fourth place, we come back here and run through the list again. That's about 20 nights altogether. We should be out of here and headed to Paris before then."

"And then what?"

"I don't know," Leon said.

"I mean, what are we doing? What are we doing here? What are we going to do in Paris?"

"We're fighting the fucking Germans, and we're going to keep fighting the fucking Germans. What's the matter with you?"

"But are we?" I said.

"Of course we are. We take risks—"

"To what end?"

"We blow shit up," Leon said. He was getting worked up. "We slow them down. We occupy their attention."

"But do we really make a difference?" I said.

"What's gotten into you?"

"Do I really have to tell you?"

Losing Manon had changed everything for me in many ways, but it had also changed nothing. I had nothing to show for a fight I continued to engage in, nothing but the loss of the only real love of my life. Because we weren't slowing the Germans down, not really. We were just a damn sideshow. The real war was in Russia, and it wouldn't come here until the Americans did. Until then, the Germans were just killing time and we were shooting slingshots at them.

Oh, and listening to the radio. Trying to ignore my rant, Leon had turned on the set. It warmed up quickly, and soon the familiar voice was speaking: de Gaulle. It wasn't one of the radio addresses he used to give from London. He was in Africa now, and there was a cheering crowd that sometimes drowned out the words.

I heard the words "punish" and "traitors" as the signal faded in and out, then, "those so-called leaders who rushed headlong into capitulation in June 1940, who used the disaster to strangle liberty, who delivered themselves to the Germans under the symbol of collaboration, who played France for lost."

Then de Gaulle said France "must track down those who betrayed her, admitting no pretext of pardon... France must raise the sword of justice."

Again, there was a lot of cheering. And all I could say was, "See, all he gives a shit about is getting even when it's over."

"Don't you want to get even?" Leon said.

"I want it to be over first. That's what we should be concentrating on, what—"

"Shhh."

De Gaulle was still speaking. "At the moment most useful to the Allies, French Resistance, organized at the cost of sacrifices, will be engaged in force against the enemy and his accomplices."

"You see?" I said. "But what about in the meantime?"

I snapped off the radio.

"We need to kill more Germans," I said. It just fell out of my mouth, but I meant it.

"You were always the careful one," Leon said "You were the one who wanted to think things through. You liked order. Now you just want to close your eyes and kill Germans. That can't be how this works. There has to be at least some order to what we're doing, and these people, they have some order about them."

"They aren't about fighting and you know it."

"Come on, they fight."

"That's bullshit," I said. "They conduct operations, quote unquote. They await instructions, quote unquote. They basically blow up a few rail trestles and build their bureaucracy and wait for the goddamned Americans — and then they figure they and their almighty bureaucracy will be in place to take over after the Americans are finished mopping the streets."

"You've really been thinking about this." Leon was almost whispering.

"It's all true and you fucking know it," I said. "The real fighters are out there in the hills. They're the ones in a war. They're the ones who are doing what it takes, killing fucking Germans. They want to win."

"But they're reckless. You know it. I know you, and you know it."

"You used to know me," I said.

"I've always known you."

"But since Manon—"

"I know you better than anyone. And this isn't you."

"Get used to it. It's the new fucking me," I said.

9

Everybody knew where two buildings in Limoges were: the Benedictins train station and the Saint Etienne Cathedral. To me, Benedictins was the more important because it was kind of a North Star. In many places in the city, all you had to do was turn on your heel until you saw the clock tower, and that would orient you properly — a real boon to a newcomer. The cathedral was different. You knew about it just because, well... just because.

So there I was, sitting on a bench outside of the cathedral, trying to look holy. That this was an acting job for me went without saying, but I had seen it all before and thought it wouldn't be that tough to pull off. You sat on the bench, leaned forward, and alternated holding your head in your hands and looking down at your shoes with an occasional peek up at the majesty of the architecture. The look on your face had to be a combination of pain and searching. For me, on that day, it wasn't hard — because the whole thing was such infuriating bullshit.

I was a few minutes early for the meeting with my contact, so I felt forced into this public interpretative dance. It was at midday, and the square outside the church was not busy, not exactly, but it wasn't far from empty. It was lunchtime and more than a few people took whatever they carried in their meager sacks and sat in the sun in the botanical gardens behind the church. There was a smaller number, some carrying those meager sacks, who stopped in for a few kneeling words with the almighty either before or after eating — praying for peace, or a peach. Because for most people, that's what this war meant: not death or despair, just hunger.

There were a thousand places in Limoges where I could have met the contact who was supposed to tell me about my next mission — but this is where the bullshit came in. We could have met in a movie theater because they were always crowded, full of people escaping life for a few hours to watch some of the light comedic crap that tended to be on offer. It was as if the Nazis encouraged it. Just keep them laughing.

So we could have met there, or at the counter of a hundred bars over a cup of fake coffee, or in a food line outside of a vegetable store, hoping for a few spears of asparagus while knowing instead that all that was going to be left when we reached the front of the line was rutabagas. Real life in Limoges provided an infinite number of possible meeting places that seemed real and natural. Hell, the guy could have just sat down next to me on the bench. But no.

Instead, we had to go through this nonsense — overly organized, dreamed up by people in charge of dreaming, full of complex maneuvers and details that could only have been invented by a bureaucrat. They liked to think they were Resistance fighters, but that's what they were: bureaucrats. They made plans. They gave orders. They built an organization. Fighting was somewhere below that on their pecking order, and it became more obvious every day.

The church bells rang briefly on the half-hour and it was my signal to begin the stupid dance. Into the church I went, through the door on the right. Just inside was a big statue of Saint Etienne in a small lobby — at least I figured that's who it was. I had neither the time nor the inclination to make a more definitive determination.

And now the cloak-and-dagger bullshit really began. I was to enter the main area of the cathedral through the door on the right. I had been in a few big cathedrals before — the Stephansdom in Vienna, and the big job in Cologne — and they were all a variation on the same idea. They all had a massive main altar fronted by acres of seats. In Vienna, the seats were benches. Here, they were individual wooden chairs, hundreds and hundreds of them. Then, around the perimeter of the building, pretty much starting at the front door and all the way to the back, even continuing behind the main altar, were a dozen or more chapels, small altars with maybe a dozen or so chairs, each dedicated to a different saint or something.

I was supposed to meet my contact in the third chapel on the right. There was supposed to be a confessional box there, and I was to go inside and kneel down. My contact would be seated in the priest's spot. He would tell me what I needed to know, but there was no way he would be able to absolve me of my disdain for the whole stupid rigamarole.

As soon as I got inside the main church, I had a problem. I was supposed to go to the third chapel on the right — except that the first thing you came to on the right side was an area containing the baptismal font. So did that count as the first chapel, or did I begin counting with the next one?

As I stood there and tried to decide, I saw a shaft of light quickly flash in the distance as a door from the outside was opened and closed. I was in the back right of the church and the flash came from the front left, a couple of hundred feet away. Standing there was a Gestapo officer, and an observant one at that: he'd removed his hat.

I don't think he saw me because it was dark, especially in the back and around the sides, and because there were pillars arrayed to provide cover. But I needed to make a decision, and I decided to keep going. I was here to have my confession heard and that would be my story if the German came upon me. I decided to skip the baptismal font and began counting after that — one, two, three chapels. A little sign said it was the chapel of the two Saints-Jean. To the right, there was a wooden confessional box. I went in. I tried to take a quick peek over my shoulder to spot the Gestapo man, but I did not see him.

The panel between me and the priest slid open. Then came the final bit of cloak-and-dagger bullshit, my recognition code. I recited it in an almost sing-song of contempt: "Bless me father for I have sinned. It has been 11 weeks since my last confession..."

"Good, it's you," came the reply.

"That's not the recognition code."

"I don't have any time for that stuff."

"Are you really a priest?" I said.

"Yes," he said. "So I like to think I know what's important and what's — you should excuse the expression in here — bullshit."

This was a priest I could deal with. He made it quick. I was to take a train the next day and get out at the Brielle station. Before getting on, a suitcase would be waiting for me at the left luggage desk. It contained fuses and timers. At the station, after dark, rail workers would meet me and take me to the job. He handed me the ticket I would need to claim the bag at the station.

"You got it?" He seemed in a hurry.

"One thing," I said.

"What?"

I told him what happened to Manon and what I was feeling, the despair and the rage. I hadn't been to confession since I was a kid but it felt good, just expressing my feelings out loud. I probably talked for five minutes straight without stopping about how I wanted revenge somehow. The priest never interjected, waiting until I was done.

"Are you looking for absolution?" he said.

"I honestly don't know."

"Let's try this," he said. He asked if I remembered the Act of Contrition. He began it, and I found myself able to follow along, mumbling from memory. When we were done, we recited an Our Father and a Hail Mary together.

Then he said, "You are absolved of your sins. But just know this: You are a soldier fighting in a war. Killing soldiers in such a situation is not a sin. I cannot heal the grief you feel for your wife, but I hope I can clear your conscience of the rest of it. You are a soldier fighting in a war."

I thanked him and shoved the claim ticket in my pocket. I actually felt better as I left the confessional box, turned left and headed for the exit. It was only then that I heard the footsteps behind me, leather slapping the stone floor. It was the Gestapo officer. But when I looked quickly over my shoulder, I could see that he wasn't looking at me. Hat in hand, he was entering the chapel of the two Saints-Jean and taking my place in the confessional.

10

I didn't know what I was anticipating at the left luggage counter — a wink, a whisper, something — but there was nothing. I handed the man the claim check, he handed me the bag, and that was it. He was back in his chair and resuming his nap before I had even managed to turn and leave. I shook the bag, which wasn't heavy, and neither felt not heard anything. The timers and fuses and detonators were likely wrapped up in a couple of rolled-up shirts.

My train ticket was for Brielle, about a half-hour north of Limoges. It was late in the afternoon and the Benedictins station was somewhere between empty and crowded, although I'm not sure it ever really got crowded anymore. My story was simple enough: a visit to a sister who had just had a baby. A small wrapped gift completed the tableau as I sat on one of the benches. If one of the Gestapo men stopped me for a chat, he could shake the box and hear the rattle.

To lessen the chance of one of those Gestapo chats, I sat next to an older woman and immediately engaged her in conversation. She was headed one stop farther than I was on the same train, to Bellac. She was visiting her sister, who was recovering from pneumonia. I practiced my story about the new baby, she enlightened me on the significance of various colors of mucus that her sister was coughing up, and it was all very pleasant. It also worked: two Gestapo men entered the station from the doors right beneath the clock tower, scanned the waiting room quickly, and left within seconds.

My stop, Brielle, was a nothing kind of place, a crumbling concrete platform. There wasn't a true station building — it was more of a hut that could hold the ticket seller and maybe a half-dozen people if they needed protection from a downpour. But I couldn't imagine a half-dozen people ever gathering there at the same time. The town, which was across the street from the platform, consisted of a half-dozen small wooden buildings. One well-placed match and Brielle would be down to a pile of ashes and the concrete platform. I wondered who might notice, either way.

I had about an hour to kill and debated my options. Part of me thought that waiting alone at the station made the most sense. The problem was that the hut was locked, and I would be a tad conspicuous, seeing as how the schedule tacked to the hut indicated that the next train wasn't for four hours. It would not be the easiest of explanations if one of my German friends came upon the scene.

The alternative was to go into the town, as it were, and find something to eat. On the plus side, it was exactly what a traveler might do. On the minus side, it would show my face to whoever might be in the town's cafe, which could be a problem if the Gestapo came looking after our little explosion took place. On the plus side again, it wasn't as if the Gestapo would be walking around with my picture — there were a hundred locals who were more likely on their radar when the subject turned to acts of sabotage. And besides, I was hungry as hell.

As it turned out, the cafe was beyond good — at least by war standards. Only the owner, an older couple and I were there, and the only item on the menu was listed simply as "stew," but it was superb: carrots, potatoes, peas, onions, a bit of asparagus, and two actual pieces of meat, all swimming in a creamy but tangy gravy. Oh, and wine and bread — although it was a little stale, and I had to pick out a few small pebbles of unrefined salt. Still, this was a real meal, and I mopped up every last bit of it with the bread.

"Chicken?" I asked. The owner had come to top off my wine and take the plate.

"Veal," he said, in a whisper. "One of the advantages of living in the middle of nowhere. I have a tiny patch that I farm, hidden back behind the trees. Most people here do. If a German ever comes in, he gets the usual shit: rutabagas, Jerusalem artichokes, maybe a little carrot. But only one has ever been here. I'm pretty sure he was lost."

"Well, this was an unexpected pleasure," I said. He told me what I owed him and said he would need a couple of ration tickets, for show. I pulled mine out and shuffled through what was left.

"One square for bread, one for rutabagas — that'll do it," he said. In his apron, he carried a small pair of scissors, the same kind that merchants wore on a string around their necks.

"No ticket for the wine?"

"No, I make that myself."

"Again, this has been wonderful."

"Glad to be of service," he said. Then he pointed with his right arm. "And now, what you want to do is walk that way about a mile. There will be a small shack there that looks as if it should have blown over in the last storm. Paul will be inside."

I looked at him. Paul was, indeed the name of my contact. I had already been given directions to the shack by the priest.

"There aren't a lot of secrets here," the cafe owner said, with a small smile. "Besides, I think you're carrying the exact same suitcase as the last guy."

I walked in the dark. The shack was there and Paul was there, along with two others. They were all rail workers. They were locals who knew the equipment and the weak spots in the security. This was going to be a simple job, blowing up a small railroad bridge. They didn't really even need me — they just needed the stuff that was in my suitcase.

"But we do want another set of eyes on the connections, after we set it all up," Paul said. "We're pretty sure we know what we're doing, but just in case."

"No problem," I said. I had learned enough about explosives in Lyon to be their extra set of eyes. But my specialty had always been the planning of the operations, and I couldn't resist asking them to walk me through what they were expecting. They did but sounded pretty annoyed.

"But what about security? I mean, you have to be expect there to be some guards—"

They stopped me with a knowing look among the three of them.

"Quit talking for a second," Paul said. "You'll see."

We piled into a beaten-up sedan and drove the last mile or so, stopping a few hundred yards from the bridge. It was a pretty dark night, but even in the light generated by a sliver of a moon, you could see the silhouette of a soldier carrying a rifle.

"You see," I said. "There's a soldier."

"Shut up," Paul said.

"But—"

"Marcel? Is that you Marcel?" Paul called out, not even bothering to lower his voice.

This was not a German soldier but a member of the local garde. They all very clearly knew each other.

"Oh, shit. Not tonight," Marcel said.

"Sorry, my friend."

Paul hugged him and took the rifle from Marcel's hands.

"What is this thing?"

"It's a fucking pop gun," Marcel said. "You couldn't stop a rabbit with it. And get this — I have to bring it back at the end of the shift."

"What time is that?"

Marcel checked his watch. "A half-hour."

"Still the same ass-backwards system?"

"Yep."

"Perfect."

"Ass-backwards?" I said.

"My friend Marcel drives out here from the barracks," Paul said. "When his shift is over, he drives back to the barracks and his replacement drives back out here. The bridge is uncovered for 10 minutes every eight hours that way."

"More like eight minutes, if my replacement is ready and waiting as he should be," Marcel said.

"Plenty of time," Paul said. And it was. There was a time when the moment of the explosion had been almost orgasmic for me. But that night, really not so much.

We were back in the beaten-up sedan when I asked Paul if Marcel could get in trouble.

"Nah," he said. "It's not his fault their system is fucked up. But this one was easy. There are others where the garde just has to make himself scarce and say he was off sneaking a drink or getting laid. They almost always get away with it. The Germans know that they can't really trust a lot of the gardes but they don't have a choice. They don't have the manpower to do it themselves."

"Not with all the men they need in Russia, I guess," I said.

"You guess correctly."

"First time for everything."

They dropped me a couple of hundred yards from the station, where I would climb into a lorry and make the journey back to Limoges as the companion of who-knew-what piled in crates in the back. Paul walked me over and said goodbye. We hugged, and I just had to ask him.

"But what good is all of this?" I said. "That blown bridge will be repaired in what? A week? Two weeks?"

"A week. Maybe five days."

"Is that really making a difference?"

"I have to think so," Paul said.

"Why?"

"What choice do I have?" he said. I handed him the suitcase and climbed into the back of the lorry.

11

This was the fourth safe house. Our "room" was a space under the eaves, the top floor of a five-story apartment building, hot as hell even on a cool night. The way you reached our perch was to climb a steep staircase hidden in a closet in one of the flats below us. That flat was also where we used the bathroom — and let's just say that the residents, the Lauriers, a nice-enough pair of fossils, would just as soon not deal with either of us clomping down the stairs for a midnight piss. So they left us a bucket with a note pinned to it: "For nocturnal emissions." Leon and I didn't know if they intended the joke or not.

The furnishings consisted of two unstable cots (along with the bucket). There were no light fixtures. I was half-dozing and Leon was reading a newspaper by the light of the moon. He was squinting so hard that it made my eyes hurt just looking at him.

"Didn't your mother tell you that you'd go blind that way?" I said.

"Yeah," Leon said. "She also told me I'd go blind another time, when she walked into the bathroom and found me scrubbing myself in the tub with, well, enthusiasm."

"So she was wrong on both counts."

"Wise woman," he said. "Loved her to death. But not infallible."

The remnants of our dinner lay on two plates on the floor — broth, bread and fake coffee. And by remnants, I meant a stray crumb or two and maybe a drop of broth. The soup was swill, the bread stale, and the coffee tasted as if it had been flavored with dirt from the garden — but neither of us cared. To be in France in 1943 was to be hungry all the time. We were happy to have what we had.

"Which rag is that?" I asked. He held it up for me to see, but as I told him, "I can't fucking see in the dark."

"It's *Sud Ouest*," he said, almost sheepishly, as if I had caught him in the tub.

"How many pictures of de Gaulle on the cover?"

"Just one," he said. I could barely hear him even though he was about four feet away.

I snatched the paper from him and held it close to my face. The picture of de Gaulle easily took up 20 percent of the square footage of the front page. There were a dozen stories on the page and de Gaulle's name was in six of the headlines. My favorite was the story about German losses on the Russian front that said, "de Gaulle Encouraged by Allied Gains in East," as if he was somehow responsible. My greatest disappointment was the inability of the editors to spin the story aimed at women to say, "de Gaulle's Favorite Rutabaga Recipe." But I'm sure they thought about it.

I liked to give Leon and the rest of them shit about it, mostly because I believed it, and this was a prime example. They were so busy creating a kind of cult of personality around that guy that they didn't really care about the rest of it, the rest of us.

"It's a very flattering pose—"

"Now listen," Leon said.

"Can't you be honest about this for five minutes anymore?" I said. "You used to be the skeptical asshole journalist. That's who you were. You used to see through shit like this in 30 seconds. But now—"

"That's not fair—"

"It is fair," I said. I threw the newspaper back at him. "Look at that fucking picture and tell me that this whole thing isn't about setting him up to be the president when this is all over."

"It's not only about that—"

"I heard that 'only.' You know it's true. Thank God, the cynical asshole is still in there somewhere."

"It's about a lot of things," Leon said. "And one of them is being smart and having a bit of military discipline and not getting people killed for no reason."

"It's a war," I said.

"It doesn't have to be a stupid war," he said.

Leon went back to reading his paper. He still hadn't figured out a way to get us out of Limoges but he was confident he'd come upon an idea once we were done with the Resistance meeting the next week in Saint-Junien. He had already warned me, though, that I was the silent partner and that he was probably not going to say much, either. It was to be a meeting of a half-dozen branches of the local Resistance, half of them probably Communists, and we were to report on our recent activities, take mental notes about the rest and get back to Limoges.

"Remember the last place we stayed in?" I said.

"You mean two nights ago? Yeah, I remember."

It had been a palace by comparison to our current spot, a two-bedroom flat with a living room and a kitchen. We could have had a party there, a big party — you know, if we weren't hiding from the Gestapo, and if we had any friends.

"Did you look around the kitchen?" I said.

"I guess."

"Did you see the dog dish?"

Leon smiled. I could tell because I could see his teeth in the moonlight. There was no dog — nobody seemed to have a dog anymore, mostly because there was nothing to feed a dog given that all the humans were going hungry — but there was still a dog dish. And inside the bowl was painted the picture of Marechal Petain, the hero of the first war, the quitter of the second.

"You saw what they did with the Marechal, right?" I said. "It's like they turned him into a god. A decrepit old man who bent over rather than fight the Germans, but a god. Our god! People in this country used to cherish playing cards with naughty pictures on them, and now we get playing cards with the Marechal on them. Our god! And, and—"

"Come on, we're nowhere near that."

"But think about it," I said. "You know how small the Resistance is. You know that 90 percent of the people in this town, right here, are for the Petain, for the Vichy. It's probably more than 90 percent. Some of it is fear. Some of it is just human nature, just calculating the easiest and safest way to survive. But some of it is that goddamn dog dish. You know it and I know it. Petain's face is everywhere. I keep repeating myself, but they've built him into a god."

"So what you're saying is, de Gaulle will be next in the dog dishes," Leon said.

"It's coming."

"It'll be awhile."

"But when it does—" I stopped when I heard footsteps on the staircase. A head popped up led by a shock of white hair. It was Old Man Laurier.

"Black car outside, two men, banging on the door for the concierge," he said.

12

I looked at Leon, unsure.

"We can barricade the closet with suitcases," Laurier said. "If I hurry, we can get it done. But if those men can count the windows..."

You like to think that you have thought of everything but you really never do. You never do. This garret was small and quiet and pretty well hidden, but the old man was right: if the Germans bothered to count the windows to the top, they would see that the last one was the one through which Leon was catching the moonlight. They would ask the Lauriers about the attic, and they would find it even if they refused to answer.

"We need to go," Leon said, and I agreed. Just like that, just on instinct — and the decision was made. We were down the stairs with our little knapsacks in 30 seconds. From the banging, it sounded as if the Gestapo men were on the second floor. Provided it took a minute or two per floor to get the tenant to open up and make a quick search, we likely had enough time.

"Thank you — and grab the plates and cups," I said over my shoulder to the old man. Hopefully he would be able to scoop them up and get them put away in time, as they were the only evidence of our visit. And with that, we were out the back window of the Lauriers' flat and down the fire escape. I don't think the metal creaked too badly as we scampered down, although every sound was amplified by my fear.

We held on to the last rung of the last ladder and dropped onto the ground without so much as a turned ankle. Then we began running toward the cathedral. I gave a quick look back when we had gotten about a block away. In the Lauriers' window, I saw a man in a black uniform pointing in my direction.

"Come on," I said, and Leon followed me. We ran about two more streets and were in front of the cathedral. I thought I heard shouting behind us and two slams of a car door. They were probably going to catch us within 30 seconds if we didn't hurry.

"Careful, careful on these cobbles," I said. We were both in our forties but we still ran like we were in our twenties, especially when being chased — although, come to think of it, Leon outran enough jealous husbands and boyfriends in his twenties to medal in the Lothario Olympics. But we were doing okay, and as long as one of us didn't stumble on the uneven stone promenade in front of the cathedral, I was pretty sure we'd make it.

Behind the cathedral were the botanical gardens, sandwiched between the church and the Vienne River. The gardens were on about six different levels, with plenty of places to sit and contemplate — the stone wall fronting the river, a dozen benches and eight or ten sets of stairs between the levels. Throughout, there was row after tidy row of plantings identified by neat little signs. But the thing was, I wasn't all that interested in either the Commelina tuberosa or the Mirabilis belle de nuit — not on a good day and certainly not on that night. I wasn't interested in sitting or contemplating.

"Just follow right behind," I said, almost in a hiss, and Leon did as instructed. I knew where the stairs were, and where I was headed. We were at least two levels below the top when I heard the Germans. I was counting on the fact that they didn't know the layout as well as I did.

At the bottom level, along one of the paths and behind what had once been an old abbey, there was a door. You might run by it if you weren't looking for it. It was down a couple of steps and framed by a little stone arch, kind of built into the landscape. It led to a series of tunnels that were beneath the abbey, when there was an abbey.

The Resistance was pretty sure that the Germans had no idea about the tunnels' existence. The door was unmarked and there was some brush growing a bit wildly nearby. To see it was not to suspect what it was. Anyway, the decision was made to leave the door unlocked unless someone was hiding inside — in which case the door could be secured by a massive iron bar. The wood was thick enough to stop the bullet from a revolver, and the iron bar was strong enough to prevent a man from opening it without a battering ram and a lot of stamina. If you arrived, and it was locked, the knocking code was two quick knocks, then a pause, then three quick knocks.

When we arrived, it was unlocked. We were inside, had located the iron bar, and dropped it into place, all within about a minute. The door was thick enough that we couldn't hear anything, but one sliver of moonlight did manage to leak through a tiny imperfection in the wood. Safe, we believed, Leon and I sat in silence.

Then: Bang. Bang.

It was two knocks. We looked at each other, and I held my breath. The pause seemed like forever, but it was probably only five seconds. Then there was another sound, not a knock but a shaking of the door handle, and then a shove into the wood, like with a shoulder. But the iron bar held easily, and that was it. We couldn't leave but we could exhale.

We got up to explore. About two steps in, Leon stumbled into a ledge built into the wall and found a candle and some matches. He lit it and it was as if a whole new world opened up. These were not makeshift tunnels but elaborate stone galleries separated by arched passageways. We didn't go that far in because the place honestly gave me the creeps, but it was quite an example of subterranean architecture. It wasn't as if they dug this thing in an afternoon.

"Holy hell," was all Leon could manage as an expression of admiration. "What do you think they used it for?"

"I think the official line is they hid people from religious persecution," I said. "The unofficial line is that they used the tunnels to store food and wine, to preserve them during the hot summers. But given that they're right beneath an old abbey, I think there's probably a third explanation, too."

"And that is?"

"I figure this is where the abbots banged the nuns," I said.

It was on that happy note that we slept, using our knapsacks for pillows and our second set of clothes for blankets. Just before I fell asleep, Leon said, "Cloak-and-dagger, brother."

"What do you mean?" I said.

"You're always talking about, and I quote, 'cloak-and-dagger bullshit'. Well, that cloak-and-dagger bullshit just saved our lives."

I didn't answer him. Hours later, when a bit of sun began to shine through the imperfection in the wood, we took a chance on opening the door. It was, as it turned out, a beautiful morning.

13

A   s it turned out, we were a threesome on the jaunt to Saint-Junien. It was supposed to be just Leon and I, but then it was decided that our ride out to the meeting with the other Resistance groups would go smoother with Martin doing the driving, given that Martin was a vice-mayor of Couzeix, and he had all kinds of credentials allowing him not only to obtain petrol but also to visit throughout the region without any real need for explanation to the Germans.

"I'm kind of a regional inspector," was how he explained it. "Day or night, I'm allowed to be pretty much anywhere. These things," he said, holding up the various passes that came with the job, "are more valuable than ration tickets."

"Especially if you're in the Resistance," Leon said.

"Yeah, but even if I wasn't. Who needs ration tickets when you can drive out to your uncle's farm and bring home a basket of vegetables and a leg of lamb a couple of times a month? Just the petrol itself—"

"And how did you qualify for this plum assignment?" I said.

Martin smiled. "Well, I could tell you that it was because of my intelligence and wit and service to the community — all of which are true, by the way. Or I could tell you that it was because I am married to the mayor's eldest daughter. I will leave it to you to decide which was more important."

"And does the mayor know?" Leon said.

"About this? The Resistance? Yes and no. He's in a bad spot — all the mayors are. The Germans are up his ass constantly, and when they aren't, Vichy is. They want to make their STO numbers, to get their almighty free workforce for the Fatherland. But on the other hand, he has the people of the town to consider — and every 18-year-old boy is hiding in some cave right now rather than going to work in Germany, and he feels like he'll be betraying them, betraying his people, if he searches too hard in those caves. Then there's his police force, half of which is spying for the Resistance, the other half for Vichy — and even if he can guess, he isn't 100 percent sure who is spying for who. It's an impossible situation."

"It sounds, well, like you said... impossible."

"He's a good man," Martin said. "But I swear, he drinks his dinner every night. And I don't think he sleeps. Every time they hand over a kid to the militia for STO transport to some munitions factory in Dusseldorf, he cries. He literally cries. And then he deals with the crying parents. And then the next day he deals with the Gestapo captain demanding more kids. It's a nightmare."

"So what does he tell you?" I said.

"The only time we ever talked about it, we didn't really talk about it. He just looked me in the eye and said, 'Just protect my daughter.' That was it. So he knows, but he doesn't know."

"And your wife?"

"She knows I'm bringing home a ham tomorrow," Martin said. "That's about it."

We drove north, or maybe northwest. The built-up part of the city gave way pretty quickly to some farms and then a bunch of nothing. I didn't know where the official border between the city and the next town began but we had to be past it. It was just a dusty road through empty land — until, in the distance, a dark smudge on the landscape grew bigger and then came into full focus. It was a military vehicle, a German patrol.

"All right," Martin said. "Show time. If he asks for your identification, just hand it over. But I do all the talking."

"Jawohl," I said.

"Not funny," Martin said.

"A little funny."

"Shut up."

Martin and I were sitting in the front seat with Leon behind us. We didn't have a weapon. This was all going to have to be accomplished with Martin's charm and with his magic paperwork. I wasn't great at trusting anybody to do anything for me, but I didn't have a choice here. Leon and I really were just passengers in this one, literally and otherwise.

We pulled up to the soldier and, before he even said anything, Martin handed over his passes. He had explained during the drive that one was his identification as vice-mayor, another was his petrol permit, and the most important was his universal travel permit — all territories, all hours. The soldier studied them and handed them back.

"Can I ask your business, sir?" the soldier said.

"Fairly routine, corporal. A work detail to retrieve a captured printing press and the accompanying paper and ink. Fewer Resistance newspapers for them, more supplies for our small town. Hopefully, we can fit it all in here."

"So you're not going to the quarry?"

"No, no, out farther than that. Much farther — to an abandoned logging camp past Saint-Junien."

"Ah, good," the soldier said. "Safe travels then."

And with that, we were gone. The paperwork truly had been

magic. A few miles along, there was a turnoff to the left with a small sign and an arrow: QUARRY.

"What's that all about?" I said. "Why was the soldier asking about the quarry?"

"We think it's an execution spot," Martin said. His manner was matter-of-fact. He never took his eyes off the road ahead.

"Jesus," I said. "You think it's an execution spot? What do you mean, you think?"

"I mean what I said. We think it's a place where the Gestapo in Limoges takes people after they're done wringing information out of them. We followed a lorry from Place Jourdan out to here once and it took the turnoff."

"But they didn't follow them?"

"No," he said. "Another time, we had a man out here by the road and he heard what he believed to be rifle fire. But there are all kinds of explosive sounds at a quarry—"

"There's a difference between rifle fire and dynamite, for God's sake—"

"But there is also hunting in the hills around here, and the sound can ricochet."

"You just don't want to know," I said.

"Alex, come on," Leon chimed in. The new Mr. Fucking Reasonable. I did my best to ignore him, and Martin was finally making a bit of eye contact with me as he drove.

"Do you ever try to stop them?" I said.

"We're still gathering information."

"You don't think there's a hurry?"

"We can only do so much".

"I'm sure the poor fuckers they're lining up against the stone walls are thinking the same thing," I said.

"Alex, come on." It was Leon again.

"Is that all you can say?"

We drove the final hour in silence.

14

I had, against all odds, managed to hold my tongue during the entire Resistance meeting. It was in the schoolhouse in Saint-Junien. The spokesmen for the six Resistance groups sat in children's desks formed into a circle, appearing equal parts uncomfortable and ridiculous. The rest of us sat on the floor against the wall. Martin drove the five miles to his uncle's farm and said he would meet us back at the school in two hours.

If someone was in charge, I couldn't tell. The meeting was a snooze, unless you were interested in the unspoken game of "no, mine's the biggest" that the six of them were playing at their little kiddies' desks. To be fair, Leon was only listening and not really participating, but I wasn't much interested in being fair to Leon at that point. But as for the rest of them, it was all political maneuvering and not a lot of coordination. It honestly seemed as if they were only meeting so that they could make a record of their cooperation if one became necessary in the future.

They took turns detailing recent sabotage missions — Leon's only real contribution to the meeting was the recitation of my recent bridge job in Brielle — and then they settled on a new set of radio codes in case there was the need to send an urgent message. There was talk of an upcoming parachute drop of supplies from the British — exact details to follow — and the need for a plan to distribute the goods once they arrived. And that was about it, other than the chest-puffing and unspoken mistrust.

The whole thing took an hour. As it turned out, Martin was already back from the farm when we walked out of the school building.

"So soon?" Leon said.

"My uncle had company," Martin said. His grin was the only explanation necessary.

"But you got your ham, right?" I said.

"It was waiting on the front porch of the farmhouse with a note. And I grabbed this for my trouble," he said, holding up a bottle of Armagnac. "I mean, it wasn't as if he was going to interrupt what he was doing to stop me from taking it."

Three guys from one of the Communist Resistance groups had followed us out of the building. One of them saw the bottle, wedged himself in between Leon and I, put an arm around each of our shoulders and said, "Ah, my brothers."

We looked at each other and shrugged. And so, the six of us sat down on the playground benches behind the school and passed around the bottle. Our new friends said they were from the immediate area.

"But we move around a lot," the spokesman said. His name was Ronny. "Right now, we're in an abandoned farmhouse. It's actually pretty good — there are 12 of us and six beds. The other six sleep in the barn, but it's clean enough, and the hay is pretty comfortable to sleep on."

"How do you decide who gets the beds?" I said.

"When Granite chooses to sleep in the barn, it's hard to complain or make much of a fuss either way."

Granite. He must have been the leader of the cell. Some name, that.

"Why isn't Granite here for the meeting?" I said. I felt ridiculous just saying it, Granite.

"Because he couldn't be bothered. Calls this stuff, and I quote, 'bureaucratic bourgeois bullshit.' And after experiencing it for the first time, I can't say I disagree."

We drank and talked about our business, as if we were six traveling salesmen in a hotel bar. But unlike those traveling salesmen, our topics were not the declining profit margins on damask, or some outrageous expense account story, but the growing scarcity of fuses and detonators.

"We can get dynamite, all kinds of explosives, no problem," Ronny said. "But the detonators—"

"Same with us," I said. Then I told him about the last mission, and how my sole job was to make just such a delivery.

The more we drank, the more animated Ronny's conversation became. He looked at us and said, "Look, I don't want to insult you..."

"Go ahead," I said. I looked over at Leon and Martin and their expressions didn't change. And with the opening I offered, the words burst from Ronny as if from a water hose.

"You don't like us, we don't like you," he said. "You don't like us because we're Communists and we don't like you because you hate Communists. You want to be in charge, we want to be in charge. That's natural enough. It's not going to change. And I'm actually okay with it."

Ronny stopped. He grabbed at the bottle and took a long drink.

"Look," he said. "We're rivals. We're always going to be rivals. But we have the Germans in our homes right now — why won't you fight them?"

"We do," Martin said. I had expected Leon to defend himself, given that he had played the same song for me.

"You don't and you know it," Ronny said. "You just wait. You just blow up a few things and wait for the Americans. Well, what if they don't come? I can't live my whole life with these fucking animals in charge. How can you?"

"We fight," Leon said. He was a little drunk and his voice was raised. "We fucking fight. But what's the purpose of getting innocent people killed?"

"They're soldiers, they're not innocent," Ronny said.

"That's not what I'm talking about, and you know it." Leon was talking about the reprisals. It was how the Germans tidied up the jails — three prisoners executed for every German killed tended to be the going rate, but it could end up being 10-to-1 if some Gestapo captain woke up one morning with a headache.

"It's a war. People die." Now Ronny was yelling.

No one answered. The tension ebbed almost as quickly as it had risen. Ronny was still holding the bottle, and he took another drink, a long one.

"It's a fucking war," he said, this time not much above a whisper.

15

The bottle was just about done. Leon got up for a piss and I went with him.

"I usually handle this kind of thing myself," he said.

"I have to tell you something."

"Oh, shit."

"What do you mean, 'oh, shit?'" I said. "You don't even know what I'm going to say."

"You want to go with them, right?"

"How did you know?"

"Come on, Alex," he said. "I've known you since you were 17. You've changed a lot, especially lately, but I know you. So why?"

"You know why."

"I know what you've been saying," Leon said. "And I know everything changed for you..." He stopped, seeming to search for the right words, and then just settled for what it was, blurting out, "Everything changed for you after Manon. But these guys? Be honest with yourself. You're falling in love with an idea here but ignoring the reality. It's like you're chasing a skirt—"

"It's more than that."

"Is it? Is it really? In our whole lives together, until just the last couple of months, I had never heard you call them just plain 'Communists.' It was 'fucking Communists,' or 'fucking Reds.' Always."

"Not always," I said.

"Always. You're lying to yourself."

"It's different now."

"So you believe in — what did you always call it — 'that Bolshevik bullshit?'"

"I believe in fighting Germans," I said. "And these people are my only option."

"That's not true," Leon said. "We'll be in Paris in a week — two weeks tops. We'll have many more options there. More time to think. More time to plan, to be smart about it. You can work with bigger people there to change things."

"Or I can stay here and fight."

I had been thinking about this for weeks — not this moment, not this playground circle around a bottle, but this idea. This wasn't just emotional vengeance. This was reasoned. It made sense. The Germans needed to be made less comfortable. They needed to feel that there was a cost for occupying France. It had all been too easy for them. They took our food, they took French boys for free labor — it had to stop. They had to pay. More importantly, they themselves had to feel like there was a cost. They were a race of ledger-keepers and they needed to see some entries in the debit column.

"You know, this isn't just since Manon," I said.

Leon just looked at me. Then he shrugged.

"This goes back probably two years," I said. "It was way before the Gestapo came to Lyon. She had just started the newspaper. I'm not sure if I had been on a demolition assignment yet. But we were listening to the radio, to a de Gaulle speech. And he said — and I'll never forget it — he said something like, 'There's no point in provoking all of these reprisals. There are tactics in war, and the tactics in our war must be directed by those in charge — by me and our committee. The order I give is not to randomly kill Germans.'"

Leon was impassive, just listening. He looked sad or maybe just tired. We were all so tired.

"Yeah, it was just that plain," I said. "It half went over my head when he said it but Manon jumped all over it. She couldn't believe it. It didn't really affect us — like I said, the Gestapo hadn't come into Vichy at that point — but she was really mad."

"I bet that was entertaining," Leon said.

"Yeah," I said. "She spent the next week calling him 'No-Balls de Gaulle.'"

It was getting late. I heard someone whistle, looked over my shoulder, and saw Martin. He was pointing at his watch.

"You know, the Americans are coming," Leon said.

"So you say."

"I don't know if it's tomorrow, or next week, or next year — but they are coming. That will change everything and you know it."

"I don't know it," I said.

"And here's the other thing — and you know this, too. The Germans will never leave because they know the Americans are coming, too. And they know the only way to keep them out is to stop them on the beaches here."

"That's not completely true — they're already starting to come through Italy. The Brits, too. If we make it hard enough for them, maybe they decide to withdraw and fight it out someplace else."

"But the point is, you know they're coming — through Italy, through France, through wherever," Leon said.

"It could be years," I said.

We were just sitting on a log at that point, staring into the edge of some woods. I heard what Leon was saying, but I had made up my mind. The status quo was intolerable to me. A couple of blown-up railroad tracks did nothing to change anybody's calculus — and it pissed off at least some of the locals, besides. Blown-up tracks didn't just mean interrupting German shipments, it meant interrupting trips to Aunt Marguerite's house, too. Most of the French people didn't support what we were doing, anyway. We were accomplishing nothing. That needed to change.

Suddenly, Leon stood up.

"Well, let's go tell them," he said.

"What?"

"That they have two more recruits," he said.

I just looked at him. I think my mouth was open.

"No," I said. "This is about me. It isn't about you. You don't agree with me, I know you don't."

He looked at me for maybe 10 seconds and then he just shook his head.

"I think you're wrong, but I'm not going to leave you now," Leon said. "Among other things, Manon would kill me."

His voice caught. He stopped, gathered himself.

"I know you've been thinking about this, like I said. It's not a total shock to me, so I've had time to consider what to do. And I'm doing it. And I really don't want to talk about it anymore."

I had tears in my eyes as we walked back. When we told them, Ronny was first shocked then embarrassingly emotional. He hugged us and cried and refused to let go. Then he looked at Martin, asking without asking. Martin's face suggested he was half bewildered and half incredulous. I answered for him: "No, he has important work to do in Couzeix."

Martin walked to the car and returned a minute later with a package wrapped in butcher's paper. He handed it to me. "I knew you were trouble," he said. Then he grinned.

"What is it?" I said.

"A leg of lamb. My uncle won't miss it. Well, I take that back. Unless he has a lot more stamina than I think, he's likely to have missed it by now, that and the bottle. But what can you do? Like your new best friend says, it's a fucking war."

PART II

16

The walk through the woods to the maquis' camp was five miles, give or take. It should have taken us two hours, give or take, but given the inebriation level of my new best friend, it was closer to five. It was about midnight when we emerged from the trail at the abandoned farm, greeted by a rifle and then a call for reinforcements. In other words, Leon and I didn't receive the same sloppy hug from the sober members of the group, even as Ronny attempted to make our case.

We were escorted — not at the point of two rifles, but by two men carrying rifles pointed at the ground while they located the triggers with their index fingers — to the barn. It appeared to be in pretty good shape, painted within a year or so, as did the farmhouse. I wondered why the place had been abandoned. It could have been as simple as dead parents leaving the place to their two sons, and the sons having been scooped up for the STO.

There were no animals inside the barn, just a series of makeshift straw beds arrayed around the perimeter. A small table and three chairs were in the center, beneath the sole light bulb. It hung from a long wire that dropped from the roof, and it swayed ever so slightly. In one of the chairs, a man was seated and casually reading a newspaper I didn't recognize. My suspicion was that he was Granite, the leader, a suspicion that was quickly confirmed.

Granite motioned, and Leon and I sat across the table from him. He got up and took our friend Ronny outside for a chat, leaving us for a few uncomfortable minutes. Our shadows beneath the single light bulb were eerie, frankly, and I couldn't quite make out how many men were eying us up from the straw piles along the walls.

The barn door opened. I saw Granite hug Ronny and kiss him on both cheeks. I heard him say to Ronny, "Don't ever change, you fucking romantic asshole." They hugged again, the barn door was closed, and then Granite was sitting again in the remaining chair. If the men with the rifles were nearby, I didn't see them.

"So it seems you have met my chief of recruitment," he said.

"That's not exactly how it went, Granite," I said. "You are Granite, right?"

He laughed a lot more than the question would have predicted. Laughing with me, laughing at me — I had no idea.

"Call me Maurice," he said.

"So what's with Granite?"

"It's what they call me behind my back," he said. "It started a while ago. Not surprisingly, they had all been drinking — well, so had I. Anyway, one of the men said, 'If Stalin can be named after steel, then you must be named after something just as hard.' That's when I went to bed. I found out the next morning that, another half-bottle in, they decided on Granite. They think I don't like it, so they only use it among themselves."

"Thank God, because I don't think I could call you Granite with a straight face."

"How old are you?" Maurice said.

"43."

"And him?" Maurice gestured toward Leon.

"Same," I said.

"Does he talk?"

"Eventually."

"Well, I'm 38," Maurice said. "And as you might have noticed, I'm not sure any of the rest are even 25. We've got one who's 17. I literally held him one night when he couldn't stop crying — he pissed his pants in his sleep and he woke up screaming. I'm telling you this because I don't know what's in your head right now, but this isn't all some great romantic adventure."

Maurice sat back, folded his arms and stared at us. It was clear that it was our turn to talk and his to listen.

So I gave him the five-minute version of our life stories — how Leon and I had fought together in the Great War and then grew up together in Vienna. How I had worked in sales in the family mining company, and how my traveling had led to my being recruited as a spy. How Leon had worked as a journalist and had written the story predicting the Anschluss before anyone with.

"With information that he provided," Leon said, pointing at me.

"He finally speaks," Maurice said. "And to deflect the credit. Interesting."

"Facts matter."

"I'll remember that."

I continued, taking myself to Zurich and Leon to Paris, then both of us to Lyon, where I married Manon and did sabotage work for the Resistance while Leon helped smuggle Jews out of the country. It really did only take five minutes; some life. I spent the last bit re-telling the story of the de Gaulle radio broadcast that I listened to with Manon, and my frustration with the reticence of much of the Resistance, and then Maurice interrupted.

"Are you a Communist — either of you?"

We both shook our heads. No sense lying. Maurice's reaction was to fold his arms and lean back in the chair. He pushed it back on its back two legs, back far enough that I wondered if the legs would snap from the strain or if he would lose his balance and fall backward. It wouldn't do for a man named Granite to topple at such a moment, though, and he didn't.

"Here's what I think," he said. "Well, let me back up. When I first saw you, I figured you for spies — the Gaullists checking us out, not like I give a fuck. But it doesn't add up. You're too old, first off — if they just needed a pair of big ears, they could get any kid for that. And there's two of you when they would really need only one — and one would raise fewer alarms for someone like me. And this is a dangerous business, too dangerous for somebody your age. And you're not even pretending you're Communists. So when you add it all up, you guys are too suspicious to be anything but on-the-level. To me, those are the facts." Maurice looked at Leon. "Are those the facts that matter?"

"Not a bad bit of reporting," Leon said.

"Oh, and one more thing. It's you, the quiet man, the reporter. You can't hide your skepticism. I like that."

"Why?" Leon said.

"Because it's honest," Maurice said. "I'll take honesty as the most important trait in this business, even more than courage or proficiency with a rifle."

He stood up and walked in a slow circle around where we were sitting. It was as if he was rehearsing a speech or a classroom lecture. He made the full circle and then stopped, putting one foot up on the seat of his chair and pointing at us. His eyes were wide and shooting out some kind of emotion — anger, defiance, I couldn't decipher it until he began speaking. It was definitely defiance.

"I'll tell you what I tell the rest of the Resistance," he said. "We'll go to your damn meetings because we've been told to go to your damn meetings, but we're free agents and we don't care who knows it. We don't play well with others and we don't give a shit if they give a shit. Got it? We stay up here, we go down into Limoges if it suits us, and we do what we want. If they want to help us with their British guns, fine. We're happy to have them. If they don't, we'll just fucking steal the guns we need from the Germans, or the militia, or whoever."

Maurice stopped. He took a deep breath.

"But no one tells us what to do. Got it?" he said.

Maurice didn't wait for a reply. He dismissed Leon and I with a wave toward two piles of straw in the far back corner of the barn. As we walked away, he resumed reading his newspaper, hunched over the little table beneath the single glowing bulb.

17

The next morning, Maurice introduced us to the rest of the group and they tested us on their weapons. They had two German machine guns, but neither Leon nor I had ever seen one, no less fired one. Leon did okay with his turn but the kick stunned me a bit, even as the gun was propped up on a stand in front of me. I mostly ended up shooting the top branches of the trees before corralling the thing.

I was better with the rifle, better than Leon, likely better than almost all of them. I had been a good shot as a kid in the army and, as it turned out, I picked it up again pretty quickly. The weapon felt natural, cradled in my arms. They had been laughing after my machine gun follies, but I shut them up with the rifle. I actually turned and bowed at the group of them behind me when I was done.

"Asshole," one of them shouted back.

"That's my name," I said.

"I won't forget," came the shout back. And behind them, maybe 20 yards, I saw Maurice watching.

Lunch was stew out of a huge pot, served in the farmhouse kitchen. There was one grumbler — "Does it always have to be stew?" — but given that there was actual meat in it, neither Leon nor I had any complaints.

"You don't know how much better the eating is out here, outside the city," I said to the rest of them.

"We get into Limoges sometimes, we know," said the guy who had shouted at me earlier.

"You mean, 'We know, Asshole,'" I said.

"Yes, we know, Asshole."

"And what's your name? Dick?"

The rest of the table burst out laughing. In a second, so did the guy who had shouted at me.

"My name is actually Richard," he said.

The tension broken, Leon and I told a bit of our stories. People came and went from the table, including Maurice, but we were the center of attention and gave everyone a chance to see us up close. After lunch, it was mandatory nap time, as in a kindergarten. That was fine with me. It was clear we were going to be working nights — including, as it turned out, that night.

We began our walk through the woods at twilight, six of us. Two carried machine guns, including Richard. The rest of us had rifles, including Maurice, Leon and me. It would be a five-mile walk, and I must have made a face when they told me because Richard said, "Don't worry, old man, we'll be driving back."

On the way, Maurice laid out the plan. We were headed for a spot along the road to Confolens, maybe three miles from the town, a place where there was a severe hairpin turn that would require any driver to slow to 10 miles per hour, tops. "It's so severe a turn that plenty of people stall out," Maurice said.

The night's target, he said, would be a three-truck German convoy that made the nightly run from a supply depot in Confolens back to the small barracks in Saint-Junien.

"What time does it get there?" Leon said.

"It varies," Maurice said.

"Always three trucks?" Leon said.

"Usually," Maurice said.

"Men per truck?" Leon said.

"Two."

Maurice paused.

"Usually," he said.

As we walked, Leon sidled up to me and we fell a few paces back.

"Usually?" he said.

I was the meticulous planner when it came to operations. I used to insist on multiple reconnaissance trips when I was doping out a sabotage operation in Lyon. The Resistance in Lyon allowed me to do it because I was funding a lot of my own operations. But that was always my personality — careful and cautious, especially compared to Leon, who was more emotional. But I guess that was when we were younger.

"Usually?" he said again. "There was a time you never would have settled for 'usually.'"

"And there was a time your middle name was 'Usually,'" I said.

"Not like this," Leon said.

"Just like this."

Still, if this wasn't a wing-and-a-prayer type of thing, it was in the neighborhood. We were to arrive at the spot in the road, three of us hidden in the woods on one side, three on the other. The machine guns were to take out the driver and the guard on each side of the first truck, with the rifles spaced behind to take care of the next two — with the machine guns to help. And if it was more than three trucks, or more than two men per truck, well, I guess that's why we were carrying the extra ammunition.

"And what's in these trucks?" I said.

Maurice looked at me. He shook his head again.

"It varies," he said. I must have made another face because the reply was caustic.

"We aren't the goddamn Abwehr," Maurice said. "We don't have a gigantic spy network. We have two radios, both of which are fucking broken right now. We take what we know and we improvise the best we can."

When we got to the place, Leon and I were positioned on the far side of the road, the passenger side. This was the more dangerous side, seeing as how the guard in the passenger seat would have quicker access to his weapon, but whatever.

As it turned out, we waited only about a half-hour before the truck began to rumble up the road. Maurice was right: the first truck came to a virtual stop at it reached the turn and then to a complete stop as it stalled. The last thing I heard was the soldier in the passenger seat of the second lorry cursing and then laughing at the driver in front of him. I fired one shot and hit him square on his face, between his nose and his right eye.

Then it was all noise from the machine guns, and smoke, and yelling. It all went as easily as Maurice had predicted. The Germans never even had time to raise a weapon. They were all dead within 20 seconds.

The six of us each pulled a German body out of its seat and left it on the side of the road. We used their coats to mop whatever blood we could out of the lorries and dropped them next to the bodies. It was then that Maurice unsheathed a knife with what was nearly a foot-long blade and walked from body to body, leaning over and cutting their throats from side to side. He wasn't just nicking them, either, but sawing down, nearly beheading the six corpses. The rest followed him from body to body and cheered with each savage hack. I found myself joining them at the end.

Leon, though, kept a silent distance. And when we were

getting ready to take our places in the lorries and drive off, he said, "Shouldn't we hide the bodies?"

"Why?" It was Maurice.

"Why not?"

"They're dead soldiers in a war," I said. "What's the problem?"

"Why rub their noses in it?" Leon said. "It might be weeks before they find the bodies if we hide them a little. If we roll them into the woods, even 10 feet or so, they might never find them. Isn't that better for everybody?"

"But—" I started to reply, but Maurice stopped me.

"Okay, Mr. Reporter, we'll hide them," he said.

It only delayed our departure by a minute or two. One of the heads did come completely apart from the rest of its body, and Maurice kicked it into the woods like a football. There was more cheering as it rolled into the weeds.

The lorries were French, requisitioned from the locals, so they weren't conspicuous. Still, we needed to get off the road — and there was no way we could drive into Saint-Junien, or anywhere close. About a half-mile away from the hairpin, there was an abandoned logging road on the left side, its entrance covered by all manner of timber scraps and brambles and shit. But as it turned out, the camouflage could be moved by six men in about two minutes, and replaced in the same time. The logging road allowed us to circumvent Saint-Junien, and we were back at the farmhouse within a half-hour.

Inside the lorries were enough beef and vegetables to feed a dozen men for a month, along with some uniform clothing and ammunition, most of which did not fit the weapons we had. The third lorry carried a dozen jerry cans of petrol. And as it turned out, the most popular cargo was the box containing heavy socks and the four cases of Armagnac.

18

The farmhouse was a quarter-mile from the main road, which was actually a glorified goat path that was two miles from the real main road. In other words, this could never have been much of a commercial enterprise. My guess is that it was a farm that provided for the family that lived here and maybe enough for a single trip every week down into the market in Saint-Junien. It was a living but not much of one, especially if there had been a mortgage on the place.

The point was, I hadn't seen a soul pass by in two days, not a truck, not a person walking, no one. So it was with some interest that I watched the bicycle pedal up to the front door of the farmhouse, and the woman who hopped off.

The rest of the men, my fellow maquisards, put down whatever they were doing — and the truth was, at II a.m., most of them had barely pulled on their trousers after sleeping late — and hurried over to greet her, whoever she was. Some ran. The first ones there received hugs, the rest hellos, or affectionate grasps of the shoulder, so some variation thereof. Leon and I walked over and stood on the fringe of the circle. I attempted to make eye contact with her but did not succeed.

Maurice, standing at the barn door and smiling as goofily as the rest of them, waved the woman over, and she left the joyous circle to meet him. They went inside the barn but the door remained propped open. If this was to be a sexual encounter, there had been no provisions made for privacy, or for the stray, sharp bits of straw that had already made their way into most of my body's crevices.

I had noticed that Richard was a bit of a mind-reader. Either that, or my face was somehow giving away everything, like that of a destined-to-be-destitute card player. Anyway, he seemed to know what I was thinking as I watched the woman walk into the barn. He said, "It's not like that, asshole."

"Not like what?"

"Not like what you were thinking."

"First of all, you don't know what I was thinking."

"You keep telling yourself that."

"Okay, so what is it like, then?"

"It's like she's everybody's sister," he said.

"Sisters have boyfriends, you know."

"Not her and not here," Richard said.

Her name was Clarisse Morean. She was a schoolteacher from Limoges. She was carrying a small leather satchel on a strap on her back, as any schoolteacher might. But Richard said that she was a courier for the Resistance. The last time she had come out, maybe three weeks earlier, she had brought a map of all the Gestapo headquarters buildings in Limoges. He said, "There are, like, six or eight of them," he said. "I couldn't figure out why they didn't just take one big building for the lot of them, but it seems like they all want their little kingdoms. I found that really interesting."

"Interesting how?" Leon said.

"I don't know," Richard said. "But it gives you a few ideas, doesn't it? Maybe they're not quite as single-minded as we think.

Maybe they have gaps in their communications, just like we do with the de Gaulle assholes. I don't know. It's just interest. And that's the kind of stuff she tells us."

"Is it safe for her?" Leon said.

"Put it this way: safer than for a man," he said. "They don't look at women as dangerous. The best couriers in the business here are women pushing baby carriages. The problem is that you need a woman and a baby to make it work."

Within five minutes, Clarisse and her satchel were back at the barn door. Maurice hugged her, and then she began a series of what seemed to be her appointed rounds. Three of the men were arrayed around the farmyard, maybe 10 yards apart.

The first was the 17-year-old kid who had pissed himself. She sat with him in the shade of the barn, the two of them sharing a hay bale. Even from a hundred feet away, the intimacy of the conversation was obvious. The kid wiped a tear at one point. A minute later, his whole body kind of heaved, and she hugged him until it stopped. Something she said as she stood up made him laugh — then she walked about 30 feet to the next guy, whose name I had forgotten. He might have been 20, and he smiled and handed her what appeared to be a school notebook.

"She's teaching him to read and write," Richard said. "She brought him a primer and checks his homework whenever she comes."

When they were done, it was 30 more feet to a third man they all called JP. She opened up the satchel and handed him two letters. He reached into his back pocket and handed her two letters in return.

"He has a girlfriend," Richard said. "She works in a cafe in Limoges. Clarisse is their unofficial postman. Those letters are the only thing that keep him here. Oh, shit," he said, and ran into the farmhouse.

By the time she reached her bicycle, Richard was back with a small package that fit neatly into the basket in front.

"What's this?" she said.

"We've had a windfall," Richard said. "Carrots, onions, potatoes, and some lamb."

"Windfall?"

"The vegetables from the Germans," he said. "The lamb from these two."

Richard introduced us as "our two new uncles." Her smile was easy. Her manner seemed so natural. She was about 35, probably, pleasant-looking without being a beauty. Then again, she was wearing slacks because of the bike and her hair was a mess and she had been sweating. A bit of straw strayed from her back pocket. I almost reached over to pull it out but stopped myself.

"Uncle What?" she said.

"I'm Uncle Leon, he's Uncle Alex." I couldn't gauge Leon's interest but my history had always been one of deference to his wishes, at least in this department.

"Next time, maybe I'll get a chance to chat with the uncles, but I have to get back," Clarisse said. She hugged Richard and thanked him for the food. She kissed the 17-year-old on the top of his head. And then she was off, the hint of a cloud of dust trailing her departure.

Just a cloud, and then it was gone. My mind had begun to wander a bit as I watched her, wander in all the natural ways — not dirty, not overtly sexual in any way, just... normal. Suddenly, Manon's face popped into my head. I actually kind of stumbled in place, if that is possible. And then I felt like throwing up.

19

I couldn't sleep that night. This was not that unusual for me, not since Manon disappeared. I pretty much needed to drink enough to pass out most nights. Given the Armagnac shipment we had intercepted, I had ingested more than enough to do the job — enough that Maurice, not shy himself in the Armagnac department, said something about my "olympian ability" to hold my liquor. I stood up and bowed in appreciation of his compliment and nearly toppled over in the process. Maurice said, "Okay, maybe not so olympian." Still, I couldn't sleep.

It wasn't that I was thinking about Clarisse. Really, that wasn't it. The fact that my mind had wandered did bother me and left me in a guilty funk for the rest of the day, but that really wasn't it. It was just like this some nights, when those last minutes in Lyon would play over and over like a phonograph whose needle was stuck in the rut of a record.

Manon had been hidden in one safe house, me in another. The Resistance had decided that we were in too much danger and needed to be flown to England, and we had agreed, and this was the night. We would be picked up in an open field that was bordered by hedges. Our minders would provide a landing target for the little plane by shining four torches skyward. The plane would land, and Manon and I would sprint from the hedges on opposite sides of the field. We would reach the plane simultaneously, from different directions, and the plane would take off again within seconds.

That was the plan. But as the plane landed, search lights suddenly switched on. They were carried on the backs of lorries, Gestapo lorries positioned in some nearby hills. Our plan had been discovered. The lights came on as I sprinted to the plane. I saw Manon's face, just for a second, and then the gunfire began. I was hit in the right leg. I heard Manon scream. The plane took off after I fell. Leon and the others dragged me from the field as I oozed into unconsciousness, as the lights followed the plane into the sky and the shooting continued.

I was safe and recovered quickly. But Manon? No one knew.

Her body had not been found at the site — the Resistance was sure of that. The Gestapo had not arrested her — and the Resistance was pretty sure of that, partly because of the sources they had in the prison but mostly because the Gestapo was not crowing about her capture. We believed she had made it to the plane — but the plane never made it to England.

Either way, she was gone. There really was little to no doubt of that. But how? How had the Germans found out about the pickup? There were a million things that kept me up but that was the one I just couldn't shake. How had they known? It might have been happenstance, or simple incompetence. It didn't have to have been a betrayal, but that was where my mind always went. But the truth was, I really had no idea and there was no way I would ever know.

There was one more thing. The spotlights illuminated the open field, the firing began, I was hit and Manon screamed. That was the order. At least that's the way I remembered it. More than once, I asked Leon what he remembered from that night, and he was useless. It wasn't his fault — the lights, the gunfire, the mortal fear, it all combined into a chaotic stew.

"But you're a professional journalist," I said to him. "Aren't you supposed to be good at the details?"

"When the shooting starts, and you're potentially on the receiving end, nobody's good at the details," Leon said.

Still, I was sure: lights, gunfire, me being hit, Manon scream-ing. But was she screaming because I had been hit or because she, too, had been hit? On my darkest nights, that was the only I just couldn't shake. That was one of those nights.

Plenty drunk but not drunk enough to fall asleep — that was my life in a capsule. I sat up on my pile of straw, feet on the barn floor, head in my hands. The single bulb was still lit and Maurice was seated below it, reading.

"Marx? Engels?" I said.

"Christie."

"Who?"

"Agatha Christie," he said. "English mystery writer. Clarisse tries to bring me a new one whenever she comes out."

"Give you any operational ideas for the next raid?"

Maurice laughed. "Might be better than some of mine," he said. "But no. I read these to forget. You should try it."

"Wouldn't work," I said.

"Like drinking does?"

"It usually does. Not tonight, though. Not tonight."

Maurice stood up and walked over to the pile of hay that he never seemed to sleep on. He was carrying two things when he came back, a book and a small torch. "Take these over to your bed and give it a try," he said. "If you drink any more, you'll fucking kill yourself. This could be better."

I walked back to my pile of hay, switched on the torch and began reading. The author was French, but I had never heard of him. The title of the book was *Midnight in Bordeaux*. And Maurice was right. It was working. It was relaxing me. I was starting to doze off, and I began to believe that mindless fiction might be the answer — until page nine, when the wife in the story disappeared. I'm pretty sure I didn't sleep after that.

20

The next morning, I was roused from my non-sleeping fog by a commotion just outside of the barn. Two of the men were dragging a kid in from the road. He looked as if he might be 20 years old and was scared enough to wet himself. The two threw him on the ground at Maurice's feet.

"Where'd you find him?" Maurice said.

"Wandering in the woods."

"Weapon?"

"No."

"ID?"

The paperwork was handed over. By that time, I was peering over Maurice's shoulder. The kid was named Raymond Michel. He was 19, still three months from his 20th birthday. His address was listed as Ruffec, a small town less than 20 miles to the west. Maurice looked down at the kid.

"STO?" he said.

"I want to join the maquis," was how the kid replied. He sounded like he was about an inch away from bursting into tears.

"STO?" Maurice said again. He was just a tiny bit more insistent this time, demanding the truth with just the slightest shift in his tone.

"Yes. But I am here because I want to fight the Germans."

"Fuck," was Maurice's reply. Then he looked at the two who had dragged him in and said, "Get him something to eat in the house."

The greatest Resistance recruiting tool currently being employed in occupied France was the compulsory work service program. The acronym that everyone knew it by was STO. The Germans' insistence on this mandatory round-up that sent French youth to German factories had stripped every family — as well as every farm, every shop in town, every small factory — of boys in their late teens and early twenties. Anywhere between 10 and 20 percent got caught and shipped off to work in the Reich. That left the 80 or 90 percent who were hiding in the countryside. Many had presented themselves for duty to various Resistance groups throughout the country. The numbers had swelled, and many of the groups saw themselves less as guerrilla fighters and more as small armies.

Which was fine for them. But Maurice had a problem with the whole notion, one that he talked about pretty much every day at some point or another. I had already heard a variation on the same rant three times.

"Christ," he said, beginning another rant. He watched the kid who had pissed his pants being walked into the farmhouse and he shook his head.

"What am I going to fucking do with him? I mean, come on."

Maurice had his group, and he had his own ideas. He wanted to keep his numbers small. He wanted to be a guerrilla leader, not a general officer. He said, "Hit-and-run is our best option, and it's always going to be our best option. If we try to be an army, we're playing their game. We kill them, we hurt them, we annoy them — that's our best way. That's when we will be most effective. If we try to play army with them, real-live war games, battalion against battalion stuff, we get slaughtered. Because that's their game."

"Yeah, but one more won't turn us into a battalion," I said. It struck me almost immediately how easily the "us" rolled off of my tongue.

"One more, no. But 20 more? That turns us into something different than we are now. We have to be nimble. We have to be mobile. You've been lucky — we've had food the whole time you've been here. But we don't always. And you haven't moved with us yet, but that's probably coming soon. And then you'll see — sleeping outside on the wet ground, with all kinds of critters crawling all over you. And eating whatever we can find along the trail, hoping that the berries on the bush don't give us the shits too bad."

"Sounds delightful," I said.

"It's the reality," Maurice said. "And then what happens to our new mascot in there?"

"That's not fair. I mean, come on — everybody pisses themselves the first time they're in combat. I know I did, at least a little."

"It's not that he's scared. It's that he's motivated by fear. He's just trying to save his own ass. He thinks slapping a beret on his head turns him into a maquisard. It's so juvenile. He's just a selfish brat."

Maurice pulled out his wallet. He reached inside and removed a small newspaper clipping, yellowed and frayed, obviously folded and refolded many times.

"I think I read this every day," he said. "It was meant for all of these scared STO kids."

He handed it to me. It said:

So you want to escape to the maquis? Well, you may think the maquis is just a hide-out, the ideal place where you can happily wait until the end of it all, an easy life.

Think again!

Going to the maquis means a solemn commitment to the Resistance army... It's sleeping rough, going hungry and submitting to iron discipline...

When he was done refolding the clipping and placing it back in his wallet, Maurice told me that Richard and I would be driving to Limoges in the morning to pick up a radio from the Resistance there.

"We're really flying blind out here and a radio would help," he said. "When we had one that worked, we could sometimes find the German frequencies. It didn't mean much because we wouldn't understand what they were sending, but with you and Leon, if they get even a little bit careless—"

"I get it. So how do we just drive into Limoges?"

Maurice explained the setup and didn't wait to hear my reaction. He began walking toward the farmhouse and I stopped him.

"What are you going to do with the kid?"

"Part of me wants to shoot him," Maurice said.

"But not really."

"Yeah, but not really," he said. "Another part of me wants to give him a sandwich and sent him back out into the woods. It's really what I should do. But the problem is, the Germans will find him — and now he knows where we are. And while I'm pretty sure I would last 12 hours or so under torture, that kid wouldn't last 12 minutes. He'd tell them where we are, and I don't want to move just yet. This is too good a setup. We need a few more days of rest."

"So what are you going to do with him?"

"It's a farm — he can shovel shit for a few days," Maurice said. "Then we'll see what he looks like with a rifle in his hand. If he can't help us, we send him away. By then we'll probably be ready to go, too."

21

The best plans are the simplest plans. That has been true forever, and it was true in this case. It was why I held my tongue, and didn't insist upon too many details, when Maurice laid it out for me.

Twice a week, on Tuesdays and Saturdays, the farmers' cooperative in Champniers ran a lorry down to Limoges to sell its vegetables. They had several shops that were their regular customers, and they paid a good price for what was good quality produce. The truth was, given the demand, they could have commanded a pretty good price for wilted crap, but that wasn't their way. In Champniers, they sold their best stuff, kept the second-best stuff for themselves, and gave away the rest — peacetime, wartime, whenever.

On this Saturday, Richard and I would take the lorry into Limoges and make the deliveries. It was simple. We had the travel permits and the invoices from the shops. All we had to do was be in Champniers by 6 a.m. and take over the lorry from Gerald and Frank. They were the only two who were in on the deal and there was no way they were going to talk, seeing as how our first delivery would be in La Couronne, two towns over, where Gerald and Frank had made the acquaintance of two women who were not their wives. They would spend their day raising one kind of sweat while Richard and I raised another, and we would return late in the afternoon with an empty lorry, save for a small radio hidden in the padding beneath the front seat.

Gerald and Frank were both middle-aged and overweight. Frank actually waddled a little as he walked away from the truck in La Courronne.

"They're both so fucking fat," Richard said. "I can only imagine what their wives look like. Or their girlfriends."

"I almost forgot there were still fat people — only out here in the country, I guess," I said. "There weren't any in Lyon after a while. There are none in Limoges."

The ride in was pretty relaxed. There was only one thing we needed to get straight — a potential rendezvous point if we somehow got separated. Richard suggested Place Jourdan at 9 a.m. on Sunday, the next morning, just in case.

"I only picked it because we did it once before," Richard said. "Do you know it?"

"You know the Gestapo headquarters is right there, don't you?"

"There's a bunch of them. It isn't the only one, remember..."

"But I think that's the big one," I said.

"It'll be fine. Sunday morning — it'll be quiet."

With that settled, we knew there would be at least one checkpoint along the way and maybe more than one. But we had the paperwork, and we had the new potatoes and green beans and zucchini and whatever else was back there. It was a simple story. There couldn't be a problem.

And so, when we spotted the military vehicle in the distance, and the two soldiers who manned the checkpoint, I actually felt pretty calm about the whole thing. Richard was driving and he would be doing the talking, but he had impressed me as being smart and pretty quick on his feet. There really was nothing to worry about — until, that is, the soldier on the driver's side leaned into the window and asked, "Where are Gerald and Frank?"

Drunk, hungover, sick, daughter's First Communion — there were a million things Richard could have said. But he froze. He looked nervous. Truth was, he looked guilty. And very suddenly, drunk, hungover, sick or daughter's First Communion wasn't going to cut it. I literally had about two seconds to decide what to do — and we didn't have any weapons, so shooting it out wasn't going to be an option.

In those two seconds, only one thing made sense to me: the truth.

"Look," I said, leaning over to talk to the soldier. The tone I went for was dirty and conspiratorial. Thankfully, I'd had plenty of practice over the years. In my previous life, I had been a traveling salesman who babysat the owners of a bunch of steel mills that did business with my family's magnesite mine. On paper, my job was to sell them the stuff they used to line their blast furnaces. In reality, my job was to get the mill owners drunk and/or laid after the sales part of the business was completed. For years and years, in cities all over Germany and Austria, I had perfected the dirty whisper, complete with its trusted companion, the wicked smile.

"Look," I said again, gathering myself. I had made eye contact with the soldier, and he sensed where this was heading, and smiled his own dirty smile back in reply. "My friend here, he's a little reluctant to tell the truth. But I figure, what the hell? What's the point of having a good story if you don't tell it, right?

So what I'm telling you is that, while we are driving their truck into Limoges, Gerald and Frank are doing some driving of their own." At which point, I repeatedly pounded my right fist into the palm of my left hand.

"Come on — those two?" the soldier said. "Whores, right?"

"They said they were girlfriends."

"My God, Frank will fucking break her bed."

"Among other things," I said.

We all had a good laugh — Richard had relaxed enough to join in by the end — and then we were off again. I waited about 30 seconds before I yelled at him.

"What the hell's wrong with you?"

"I don't know," he said. "I just froze."

"You could have gotten us killed."

"I know. I know."

"If we get asked again, it's the same story — got it?" I said.

"Yeah, yeah — in case they compare notes."

"Exactly."

As it turned out, there were no other checkpoints. We got into the city and made the deliveries in order, and we were done by noon. Richard had memorized the address of the flat where the radio was hidden, and that would be our last stop. Other than the one hiccup at the checkpoint, the whole thing could not have gone more smoothly.

But then, as we left the last vegetable store, the last of the crates unloaded, we returned to our empty lorry to find a black car, two black uniforms and two black trench coats. Richard managed to do the talking this time, explaining our business and handing over our delivery paperwork.

"It all seems very routine," the one trench coat said. He pocketed the paperwork. "But we would like a further word."

With that, one of the uniforms was behind the wheel of the

truck and the other trench coat was escorting Richard into the passenger side door. The trench coat who took the paperwork pointed for me to enter the back seat of his black car. He rode shotgun while the soldier drove.

22

I had walked by it before but had never been inside Villa Tivoli. If it wasn't the biggest of the buildings that the Gestapo had commandeered after their arrival — and it might have been, because it was plenty big — it was unquestionably the most famous. Because Villa Tivoli was known for torture. It was a subject that tended to grab one's attention and maintain it.

Villa Tivoli faced onto Cours Gay Lussac. Across the street was a big city park surrounded by a cinder track. If you stood on the sidewalk and looked to the left, the Benedictins clock tower dominated. The station wasn't a five-minute walk away.

One of the de Gaulle boys had visited Villa Tivoli and lived to tell of his experience. The truth was, all they did was punch him a couple of times in the trunk and the kidneys. As he said, "I had some bruises that lasted a month, and I pissed blood for a week, but it was okay. It scared the shit out of me, but I lived. They didn't even ask me much. It's like they were just having a laugh."

"Because they could," I said.

"Pretty much," he said. Then he added, "You know what I'll

never forget? When you walk in, there's this grand piano. They take you through the doors and down into the cellar for the fun stuff, but first there's this damn piano. I half-expected one of the oafs to take off the leather gloves they put on before the beating and sit down for a little Chopin."

"Nocturne for Fists and Truncheons in D-minor," I said.

My new friends escorted me into the front door of the villa and there it was. The dark wood of the piano gleamed beneath the chandelier. Polishing the thing appeared to be somebody's full-time job.

"We're not savages," the black trench coat said. He noticed me admiring the instrument. "Do you play?"

"Not so much," I said.

"Pity. I wish I had more time to practice. This beautiful piano, and I barely get the chance. So busy here. So, so busy."

I wasn't shackled in any way, and the black uniform wasn't even holding me by the elbow. It was all very civilized as we walked through the doors. But instead of heading down the stairs to the cellar, we walked up one flight to what had been a small library but was now my new friend's office.

He introduced himself formally as Captain Martin Bloch and pointed me to the chair next to his fussy little desk, one that likely had been used for opening the day's invitations and writing thank-you cards by some 19th-Century minor noble. I had done this Gestapo routine before — in Cologne and in Lyon — and seen both torture rooms and offices. They each carried their own special terror. Don't get me wrong; I much preferred the comfortable chair I was sitting in to a table with leather wrist and ankle restraints — but there was never anything about the experience that didn't loosen your bowels, at least a little.

For this day, I had been carrying my old Allain Killy identification, and that was the paper that Bloch was studying as I waited. I had three sets of papers and each had its own issue. My real papers with my real name, Alex Kovacs, were the most compromised of the three — the most recent example being just days earlier, when the Gestapo came to the bar in Limoges and asked Louis if Alex Kovacs was his boarder. By contrast, the Albert Kampe papers were likely the cleanest of the three — and I desperately wanted to keep them that way. As for old Allain Killy, he was known to the Gestapo in Lyon — and any search of any list of wanted fugitives could potentially turn up the name. At the same time, I was pretty sure that Alex Kovacs was their main target, and that would be the name that appeared on the lists, with Allain Killy listed below as an alias.

The point being, they likely would red flag me with any of the three names, if they had their shit together and did the necessary digging. But I was counting on a level of boredom on the Gestapo's part, mostly because they didn't have anything on me. So that's why I went with Allain Killy.

"From Alsace, yes — I thought I heard it in your accent," Bloch said.

"You know French accents that well?"

"I don't know if you noticed, but my French is Alsatian accented, too," he said. "From our teacher in the officers' school. But enough of that. Why are you still here? Why didn't you go home?"

At the start of the war, the Germans essentially cleaned out the French from Alsace and reclaimed it as their own. The French had it, then the Germans took it after the war of 1870, then the French took it back after the Great War, then the Germans took it back in 1940. But after a while, the French were allowed to return to their homes.

"Why didn't I go back?" I smiled my best sheepish smile. "Why do men do anything? I met a woman."

"Where was that?"

"In Champniers," I said. I was in full story invention mode.

"What brought you to Limoges?"

"My job — I do deliveries for the farmers' cooperative. Twice a week."

"You make do on two days' work a week?"

"It's better than nothing, and there's nothing for me in Alsace."

Bloch had a stack of paper on his desk that he lifted and straightened, and then lifted and straightened again, each time dropping the pages on their ends, first the long end, then the short end.

"What is this woman's name?" he said.

"A gentleman doesn't tell."

"Not even to the Gestapo?"

"A gentleman, sir," I said.

For the second time in a few hours, I offered a dirty look and a conspiratorial smile as my best defense against Nazi interrogation. Bloch stared back at me, paused one beat, two beats, then broke into a big smile of his own. Part of me thought I was winning the conversation, but most of me had my doubts. But Bloch let it go.

After a few more minutes of wordplay, it was pretty clear Bloch didn't have anything. The only issue was whether he would escort me down to the cellar for some afternoon sport. As I wondered about that, and involuntarily massaged my left kidney, there was a knock on the door behind me. I turned to see the young uniform poke his head in the door, shake his head, and leave as quickly as he had arrived.

If I had to guess, Bloch had given him the Allain Killy name, and the kid had done a cursory check through whatever list of names was handy. The head-shake suggested pretty strongly that he had been unsuccessful in finding a match. Bloch again performed his tidying routine with the stack of paper in front of him, and then he picked up my identification document off the top of the stack and handed it back to me.

I wasn't going to the basement. I was just going. Bloch offered not another word — not a warning, not a dismissal, nothing. He just waved me toward the door, and I found my own way out — through the doorway, down the hall, into the entrance area, past the piano and out. I struck a single key before I left, just for the hell of it, and it echoed a bit eerily in the big room with the high ceiling. No one rushed out to reprimand me. Then I was out the front door and onto Cours Gay Lussac. I crossed the street and walked across the park and sat on a bench on the far side, a couple of hundred yards from both Villa Tivoli and the Benedictins train station.

I wasn't in a hurry, after all. I couldn't meet up with Richard until 9 the next morning — and that was assuming he was being treated as civilly as I had been. Oh, and that they gave him back the lorry.

23

I had asked for the school's address before I left the farm, on the off chance that I had some time to kill. As it turned out, it was maybe a 10-minute walk from the park, a nondescript two-story building with an open play area of equal size off to one side.

I didn't know what I expected on a Saturday afternoon, but the schoolyard was full of kids — younger kids, maybe 6 to 10 years old; I wasn't great on kids' ages, or anyone's ages. Manon used to make fun of me when we passed women on the street. She would insist that I try to guess their ages and I was way off as often as I was close. As I got past the age of 40, the difference between an 18-year-old girl and a 28-year-old had become almost indistinguishable for me. Manon used to say, "You're going to be hopeless when I'm gone."

Manon. What the hell was I doing outside the school? I stopped, looking at the kids, then saw an open window in a room overlooking the schoolyard. A light was on, and Clarisse was sitting there, correcting papers or something. I called out from the sidewalk, and my words startled her.

"It's too nice a day to be working on a Saturday," I said. It took her a second to attach my name to my face, but only a second. She began her reply with a warm smile.

"Uncle Alex? What brings you to the big city?"

"Sightseeing."

"Stay there," she said. Seconds later, she was out the door and walking over to meet me, but not before a knot of the kids shouted out her name and received a wave in return.

"You're not leaving?" one little girl cried out.

"No, just visiting with a friend," she said.

The little girl who cried out was wearing a makeshift nurse's uniform. She was playing with a handful of boys who were dressed as soldiers. I listened as they bantered back and forth. One of the kids poked at another with his "rifle," which was really a broom handle, and said, "Mach schnell."

Clarisse arrived at my side at that moment. I made a face.

"Mach schnell?" I said.

"They're just repeating what they hear."

"But they're French."

"And all the soldiers in Limoges are German, and most of these kids don't see them as anything more than glorified policemen."

"But what do their parents think?" I said.

"Let's go inside." She put her hand on my back, gently, naturally, and steered me to the door and into the classroom where she had been working.

"You ask me about the parents," she said. "You live in your own little world where everyone is in the Resistance. But it isn't like that here. Just look at what we get to work with. These are the supplies we get from the state."

There was a half-done jigsaw puzzle on one of the tables, designed for a 10-year-old, probably. It had about 50 pieces. The title on the box: "The Marechal's Christmas."

Clarisse pulled a handful of coloring books from another

drawer, all partially filled in, all with some kind of Petain theme. The Marechal on a farm. The Marechal driving a car. The Marechal climbing a mountain.

"He has quite the publicity agent," I said. I flipped through one of the coloring books and stopped at a particularly messy bit of crayon execution. The Marechal, leaning over to pet a lamb, had a purple face — and a rather untidy one at that.

"What does the Marechal say about coloring outside the lines?" I said.

"He's against it. The Gestapo is really against it."

Clarisse opened another drawer and pulled out another box. It contained a board game called "Francisque." Inside, it was just Snakes and Ladders. I shrugged.

"You have to look at it," she said. "I mean, see what they've done here. Look at the things that help you to climb to the top. There's 'trust,' and there's 'team spirit,' and there's 'solidarity.' And the things that send you back to square one: 'idleness' and 'selfishness.'"

"It seems like they've thought of everything," I said.

"So you ask about the parents. They're pretty much okay with all of this. They don't like it but they're not willing to fight to change it. They figure they'll just wait it out. And you know what they dislike most of all? It's not the Germans being in charge. And it's not Petain — they think he's doing his best to keep the Germans in hand. It's that they have to stand in line for food. Sometimes I really think that if they could get the food supplies solved that Hitler could win an election here."

"Come on, you're not serious."

"I'm more serious than you think," she said. "And in the meantime, these kids — they barely get to play after school anymore because they have to hold a place in the milk line, or the vegetable line, or someplace else. That's why I stay late on

Saturday now — it's the only time the kids are around to have fun."

Clarisse checked her watch, and I reflexively did the same. It was past 4 p.m., getting late. She straightened up her desk and closed the window, and then we were back in the schoolyard. It was then that it appeared to dawn on her. She said, "And what are you doing here, exactly?"

I laughed and explained, running through my day, from the pickup of the lorry to my Gestapo interview in Villa Tivoli. I told her about Richard and the 9 a.m. meet-up and she said, "Well, then I'll cook you dinner. But it's too early for that. Let's go for a walk first. It's such a nice day."

Just then, the warm sun and the intermittent screams and laughs of the children were drowned out by two German fighter planes that passed overhead. They weren't particularly loud or threatening, or maybe I was just jaded. But the reaction of the children was pronounced. Most stopped and pointed and talked excitedly among themselves, fascinated and thrilled. But two kids, a boy and girl, came running and crying to Clarisse, each hugging one of her legs. She bent down to comfort them, whispering something in each of their ears. After a few seconds, the planes were gone, and the tears were dried, and the boy and girl rejoined the rest.

"What was that?" I said.

"It's because of their experiences," she said. "Most of the kids are from around here. There was never any fighting here and so they see the planes as an object of fascination. Especially the boys, they love to play war, and it's like a movie for them. But these two, they're refugees. One is from Lille, the other from Rouen. They were there in 1940 when the Germans came. They saw the planes drop bombs. The little boy, he saw his house flattened with one of his brothers still inside. And both of them were in those long columns on the roads when the German planes squealed and dove low and fired their machine guns, and everyone dove into ditches on the side of the road and prayed."

"Oh my God."

"Yeah," Clarisse said. "Although I'm not sure what God has to do with any of this anymore. And the worst part is, it doesn't get any better for them. Maybe someday, but not now. And not soon, I fear."

24

"Let's cross here," Clarisse said. We were walking through a part of Limoges that I had not seen before.

"Over there," she said. She pointed to a building in the middle of the block, a building that looked very much like all the rest — heavy and imposing door, windows with false balconies outside of each, the black iron work a riot of curlicues. It could have been an apartment building full of flats, or an office building of some financial company or some such thing. It was none of those things, though.

"Gestapo," she said, actually talking out of the side of her mouth.

"Another one? How many are there? I've heard you brought a map."

"The correct answer is 'too many,'" she said. "But I don't know. I know of at least six but I'm pretty sure there are more than that."

We had already passed a long building with the old republic's motto etched in several places on its side: *Liberty, Equality, Fraternity.* It was some kind of regional government building, bureaucrats working behind thick stone walls, doing whatever bureaucrats do when the soldiers of a foreign nation are really running things, and where your own government feels the need to change the national motto to *Labor, Family, Fatherland*. I didn't know, but maybe they were the people who designed the jigsaw puzzles.

Anyway, after the Gestapo headquarters, the street suddenly became very steep and uphill.

"Last week, they took some prisoners out and walked them to the prison," Clarisse said. She pointed to the right. "It's just up there on the next street. Watching them march them up there, up the hill, all in leg irons, it looked like it was going to take an hour. It was almost funny."

"Almost," I said.

"Yeah." She pointed to the prison walls, gray cement with a door in the middle beneath a sign that said, "Maison D'Arret." Above them was a Nazi flag, hanging limp.

"But we're going to go this way," she said, and we veered to the left, away from the prison and up some steps and into a public garden of some kind. Right at the entrance was a cupola.

"It's an old Roman site," Clarisse said. "This is actually the remains of a Roman arena. I like it but I hate it."

"What do you mean?"

"I like it because it's pretty and because it's old. But I hate it because it glorifies a time when Frenchmen were under the thumb of a foreign invader."

"There weren't exactly Frenchmen back then," I said.

"I know, but you get the point. I'm just especially sensitive to the whole concept these days."

We sat on a bench beneath the trees for a few minutes, not saying much. The sun was dipping lower, and the afternoon was cooling. I asked Clarisse if she wanted my jacket but she declined.

"Tougher than I look," she said.

"You look plenty tough."

"And what does that mean?"

"It was a compliment," I said.

"I know," she said. I felt better when she smiled, and then I felt worse when I realized that I needed her smile to make me feel better. If that made any sense.

We walked a few more minutes until we came upon a green space that I sensed was only a few minutes away from the Chapel of Saint Aurelian but in a direction I had never walked before. On the far side was a monument of some sort. "Our war memorial," she said.

"My war," I said.

"And what's this?"

"This war is different. I can't explain it. I still don't know what the Great War was about, not really, but that was my war. I was young, I wore a uniform, I was part of something big. This isn't the same. This makes more sense to me, but there are none of the trappings. This is much more about fighting evil: Hitler, bad man, must be stopped, not hard to comprehend. But even with that, I feel so much more alone."

"Tell me about your war," she said. And so I did, as we sat there, taking her on a tour of my early life that ended in 1919 in Vienna, when Leon and our friend Henry and I became inseparable friends, a truth that endured until Hitler. I decided on the spot to wait on telling her the rest. I don't know why, I just did.

"Two sides, same war," Clarisse said. It was almost a whisper, and then we were silent again. I got up from the bench and walked the 20 feet or so to the foot of the monument and gave it a good study. There was undoubtedly a lot of highfalutin symbolism involved. Carved in stone were a woman holding some fruit on a plate on the top, and a shoemaker and a porcelain worker on either side along the base, and a dead soldier laid out on his back in the middle. The inscription said, "To the children of Limoges who died for France and the peace of the world."

"But where are the names?" I said. I took another lap around the back, just to make sure I hadn't missed them, and I hadn't.

"What do you mean?" Clarisse said, after my second circuit.

"On the monument. They all have names, the names of the men who died. Every one I've ever seen has names."

"Not this one," she said. "I like it better."

"But it doesn't honor the dead."

"Of course it does. But I think it's more to remind everyone that there is a life when it's over."

I wondered a lot about that — about it being over and about what there might be for me after that. We were walking again at that point, not really talking, oddly comfortable with the silence. Or at least I was.

25

Clarisse's house was over near the cathedral. I was familiar with the area, if not the particular spot. It was a house within the warren of streets on the far side of the church, and she had the entire fifth floor to herself.

"Wow, so big."

"It's a flat that I inherited from my aunt. The downside is the five floors of stairs to get here. The upside, besides the space, is this," she said, pointing to a small doorway in the kitchen. It opened onto an outside metal staircase that led to a private roof patio. I stuck my head out the door and was no sooner back inside than Clarisse was handing me a glass of wine. "Go on up — it'll be too cold in an hour. You can see the river over the rooftops. Go on, there's a reasonably comfortable chair. I'll cook in the meantime — it won't take long."

And so I went. The wind was chilly, but if you moved the chair just so, the chimney blocked it. The view of the river and the rooftops was beautifully relaxing. I was pretty sure I was asleep when I heard footsteps on the metal staircase. It was Clarisse with a wineglass of her own.

I began to stand, but she waved me back into place, choosing to sit on one of the chair's arms. We both stared off, over the rooftops, past the river. "Tell me about after the war," she said.

"Meaning?" I said.

"Meaning the last 24 years," she said. "You can make it the short version, if you'd like."

For me, the short version was: traveled a lot, made good money, became a spy, escaped the Nazis in Austria, continued on as a spy in Zurich, met a girl, followed the girl to Lyon after the war started, got married, then lost the only woman I had ever loved.

And that's exactly what I told her, all in one long, almost sing-songish sentence. I made myself sound like more of an asshole than I really was in the tone of the telling, but Clarisse didn't seem to be offended by my flippancy. She had only one question.

"What was her name?"

My reply was as quiet as her ask. We both stared off past the rooftops again. Then Clarisse stood. "Five minutes until dinner," she said, and then she was gone down the stairs.

I followed her soon after, washed my hands, and offered to set the table. As I did, and as she fussed at the stove, I asked her without looking her in the eyes, "So what about you?"

"What about me?"

"The short version is fine," I said.

"I don't do the short version," she said. She turned off two burners on the stove, pulled out a chair and sat down at the table. I joined her, and she told the story of a 16-year-old girl from Toulouse who got pregnant without the benefit of a husband, and who came to Limoges to live with the aunt she barely knew. The baby, a girl, was given up for adoption the day she was born.

"I never even got to hold her," Clarisse said. All I could think about was the baby, my baby, that Manon had been carrying.

"After a little while, the question was if I could go back to Toulouse. My aunt, who was really my great aunt, offered to let me stay, and the truth was, my family was glad to see the back of me."

Without the baby, and the attendant stigma, she was able to be placed in a school in Limoges. She studied to be a teacher, and that's what she had been doing for nearly 15 years.

"And no one since?" I said.

"Not really."

I knew about "not really." Before Manon, my whole life had been a series of "not reallys" interrupted by long stretches of "don't really cares".

When Clarisse plated the food and placed it on the table, I nearly fell over. Veal kidneys. I didn't camouflage my reaction very well, and she said, "What's wrong?"

"Nothing."

"No, tell me."

I thought about it for a second, and decided on the truth.

"I got to Lyon in June of 1940," I said.

"So right after?"

"Yes, right after. Manon and I were married soon after. But you remember what it was like — the rationing came so quickly. We didn't have much time together as a couple when food was still plentiful, still easy to get. But at the very beginning, it was. And the first big meal Manon cooked for me..." I couldn't get the rest of it out, but Clarisse could.

"... was veal kidneys," she said.

"Veal kidneys. Cooked in bits of bacon. With new potatoes. And carrots."

"I couldn't find carrots," Clarisse said.

"Where did you get the rest of it?"

"On a trip out to the country on my bicycle," she said, "Different farm, different farmer. I traded for the veal and bacon. I gave him an old, torn arithmetic primer that I had mended."

The food was delicious, but I couldn't enjoy it. Half of me wanted this to be some kind of spiritual sign, the miracle of the veal kidneys and bacon, and the other half of me was damning myself to hell for wanting it. I was twisted in a hundred emotional knots, and I had no ability to untie them, not there, not sitting at Clarisse's dining table.

So I bolted. I didn't help with the dishes. I barely said thank you. I made up some kind of bullshit excuse and I almost literally ran from the flat, flying down the five flights and into the street. I was embarrassed about how I felt, and embarrassed about my exit. I found myself running until I reached the cathedral and realized how conspicuous I looked. So I slowed down and did what I did whenever I needed reorientation in Limoges. I turned in place until I spotted the tower of the Benedictins station. I walked in that direction and took the shittiest room in the shittiest business traveler's hotel I could find. But I'm sure I didn't sleep.

The meet-up with Richard was scheduled for 9 a.m. on Place Jourdan. There was a bar there, and I grabbed a coffee and was happy to discover that it was actually more coffee than the ersatz stuff. I hadn't been able to get Clarisse out of my head for hours — Clarisse and Manon and the myriad intertwined variations of guilt and grief and desire — but at about 10 minutes before 9, the meet-up became a welcome distraction. As it turned out, Richard and the lorry were five minutes early — and that was after he had made a stop to pick up the radio and hidden it under the seat.

As we drove back, I told him what had happened to me — the Gestapo part, not the Clarisse part — and he said, "It was the exact same thing with me. I don't know what the point was."

"Where'd they take you?"

"I don't know the street name, but it was near a prison. That's where they left the lorry."

"They didn't hurt you at all?"

"Nope. Didn't touch me," Richard said.

"They were just fucking with us."

"Why?"

"Because they can," I said.

Richard asked me where I spent the night and I said, "With a whore." I asked him where he slept and he said, "Same thing." We both laughed. As it turned out, my made-up whore story was better than his real-life whore story.

We never even got stopped once on the drive back. We just dropped the truck where we first picked it up and hiked back to the farmhouse through the woods. Exactly how Gerald and Frank got home from their girlfriends' houses after we didn't show up, and what they told their wives, was their problem — but at least we were able to entertain ourselves by inventing a few possible scenarios on the way home.

26

Maurice had received the message in the time-honored fashion — with a wife, and a wife's cousin, and the cousin's next-door neighbor as intermediaries — that the mayor of Civray was requesting his presence.

Even though Civray was one of the bigger little towns in the immediate region, this was a request, not an order, mostly because Maurice possessed more weapons than the six-member Civray police force. There were plenty of small towns in Vichy that had essentially been taken over by local Resistance groups, but not Civray. Maurice wanted no part of municipal administration, even on-the-fly administration. As he said, "If I don't want to be a general, I certainly don't want to be a goddamn mayor."

Maurice, Leon and I took one of the lorries. We used back roads for everything, but especially when we were driving — because most of them weren't even on maps, and because the Germans knew that exploring too deep into the uncharted areas could only lead to more encounters with Resistance snipers. I said to Leon as we drove, "You see, not a soul. Not a patrol. Not a uniform. It's because they're afraid."

Maurice nodded his head and kept driving. We arrived in Civray essentially through the back door. It was dusk when we pulled in down the street from the city hall. As we approached the front door, climbing the steps, a disheveled man barreled out, head down, and almost knocked us over. He offered no apologies. He made no eye contact. He just kept going.

Inside, the mayor's office was the first door on the right. It was open, and he was on the telephone. He waved at Maurice to come in and pointed at the chairs arrayed around the office.

"... a few minutes," the mayor said, to whoever he was speaking.

Long silence.

"Just calm down. Here's what I'm telling you: there's a rumor some boys are hiding in the caves along the ridgeline that overlooks Lake Prune. You know, where the kids sometimes jump in when it's hot out."

More silence, listening.

"Like I said, a few minutes."

Shorter silence.

"You're welcome," the mayor said. "A few minutes."

He put down the phone.

"This is all I do anymore," he said. "Damn STO."

The mayor explained that the guy who nearly knocked us over on the way out was a local drunk of some repute. But he had heard something about some kids hiding from the militia in those caves.

"That's when it becomes my problem, when assholes like that show up," he said. "I won't chase kids. I won't send my men out to chase kids, even though half of them think it's our duty. The Gestapo comes in and asks once or twice a month, and the militia comes in, and I fend them off as best I can. But I have to show that I'm trying, even when I'm not. So that's what I just did."

"What do you mean?" Leon said.

"So our informant comes in. Like I said, I can't ignore that — he's probably in the bar right now telling everyone what he told me. I've got to save my own neck, too. Because, fuck. So he tells me and I make a phone call. It's to a farmer whose son, I know, is in hiding. I don't know if he's the one in those caves but, even if he isn't, the farmer probably knows who is — it's right near his land. So now he has a head start."

The mayor stopped, then sighed. He looked at his watch. Then he yelled, "Sergeant!"

Within seconds, a uniformed gendarme presented himself at the office door. The mayor told him about the informant and about the cave. The sergeant offered a quick salute in reply, and he was gone.

"Best case?" he said, after we were alone again. "The farmer tells the kid, and the kid gets away, but he leaves behind some evidence of hiding there — maybe some food. Or a fire that's still smoldering — that's the best. Then I have a story the next time the militia is up my ass: 'We have such a small force here, and so much territory to cover, but look how close we came to this one: the fire was still hot.'"

"And the worst case?" I said.

"Worst case, we catch the stupid fucker and he gets put on a train for Hamburg or someplace, where he will be put to work riveting battleships together or something. And then I will make another mark in this column." He pulled a sheet of paper out of his desk and pointed at the column beneath the letters TDTS.

I looked at it and shrugged.

"Too Dumb To Survive," he said. "Of course, that helps me with the Germans. But it kills me with his parents, and with the other parents. And if he was a farmhand, it kills me with the man who employed him. And if he was working on the sly in our little metal fabrication factory — we make rivets here, believe it or not — it hurts the town's main employer. He barely has enough men to keep the place running as it is."

"Sounds complicated," Maurice said.

"It's exhausting is what it is," the mayor said. He pulled a bottle from his desk drawer and filled four glasses. His toast: "To a good night's sleep."

"So why the summons?" Maurice said.

"It was more of a request — you know I like you," he said.

"It sounded urgent."

"It is — urgent for you," the mayor said.

He eased into a longish story about the two members of his police force who worked the day shift. "I don't trust them so that's why I have them work days — so I can keep an eye on them. It makes everyone else mad, but whatever."

Anyway, he'd overheard them when they were having a coffee that morning. "I didn't get it all. I'm not sure I got even half of it. But one of them very clearly said, 'The Perrault farm. For weeks.'"

"Oh shit," Maurice said.

"Exactly," the mayor said.

Maurice looked at us. "We're at the Perrault farm," he said.

Then he looked at the mayor. "Why don't you trust them?"

"Part of it is that they're the two who want to spend their days searching for STO kids. But it's more than that. The last time the militia was in here, I saw one of their guys make eye contact with one of those two. It was subtle, but it was there. And then he just happened to be gassing up our police car out back when the militia came out — their car and our car parked side-by-side. My guy leaned into an open window and had a quick chat. I just don't happen to believe it was about the weather."

The concern was obvious. Maurice had said we were living on borrowed time at the farm, but he wanted to stay as long as we could because the group needed the rest.

"You think we're too late?" Maurice said.

"I don't know," the mayor said. "But those two were working here until 4. Now, maybe they were able to make a phone call without me knowing — but I don't think so. If I had to guess, I think you're still okay now. But I'm not sure you'll be safe in the morning."

We obviously had to hurry, but the mayor poured us all another drink, anyway. We slugged it down. Maurice made the toast this time: "To a good night's sleep... but not until tomorrow."

27

The genius of Maurice was in his preparation, even if it seemed haphazard at times. As I told Leon, "I wouldn't ever want to play chess against him. He thinks too far ahead."

The distance from the farm to our new place was close to 20 miles. We would do it in the three lorries, on the back roads, but without lights — just to be sure. So it took us three hours.

We were packed in 20 minutes because that had always been the expectation. We took as much food as we could. The clothes and the canvas and the wire and the rope and the other supplies had never been unpacked after we stole it, so there was nothing to do there. As for personal possessions, no one had more than a knapsack. As it turned out, we probably didn't even take the full 20 minutes.

The new place was an abandoned logging camp, although the word "abandoned" didn't do the decrepitude justice. It was ancient, and the main cabin appeared to be a ruin, with a big hole in the roof. Still, Maurice saw promise. When I got out of the truck, I just looked around with my hands on my hips, and I guess the disgust showed on my face.

"Don't worry," he said. "You'll see."

He barked out some orders, and the group began to function in the moonlight. The roof was patched with canvas tarpaulins. The inside was cleaned out quicker than I thought possible by a dozen strong backs. And if the floors weren't clean enough to eat off, they were soon clean enough to sleep on, provided there was a tarpaulin barrier between you and the planks.

"Leon, Richard, Alex — come over here," Maurice said, the work done. "The rest of you, get some sleep. You deserve it."

The radio that Richard and I had brought back from Limoges was sitting on the front seat of one of the lorries, hooked up to its battery. Maurice was fiddling with the dials. He also was consulting what I recognized as a code key. He consulted his watch, then a map, and then his watch again. "Come on," he said. "All in this lorry. And make sure you have a loaded rifle."

Again, we were driving without lights on narrow back roads, unpaved and unkind to the lorry's axels. But it wasn't that long of a ride, maybe 20 minutes. Then Maurice did a series of forward and backward maneuvers to turn the lorry around and get it pointed back toward our new home. He switched on the radio and listened again, the code key in his hand. He still hadn't told us what we were doing.

"Okay, come on," he said. "And bring the rifles."

We followed him through the woods until we came upon a clearing that fronted on a lake. It was a big rectangle with water on two sides — ahead of us and to the right — and woods on the other two.

We arranged ourselves in a line along our side of the rectangle, maybe 10 yards apart. Before we separated, Maurice said to Leon and me, "This is what we do. On my signal, you begin firing over toward those other woods." He pointed to the left.

"But not into the woods — aim high, into the trees," he said. "Just keep doing it. And in between, I want you to yell in German."

"What the fuck?" Leon said.

"Just yell in German. Like, 'Watch out!' Or, 'Over there!' Stuff like that."

"Why?" Leon was incredulous.

"Just fucking do it. I'll fire the first shot, and then you follow up. Do you understand?"

We heard him but we didn't understand. Still, we took our places and got ready. Within a few minutes, the sound of an airplane engine seemed to fill the night. It probably wasn't that loud, except this was the middle of the night and we were in the absence of any other sound save the occasional owl.

But then the sound was gone, as quickly as it had arrived. I still had no idea what we were doing. That's when Leon stage-whispered in my direction a single word: "Look." When I did, although the moon was not nearly full and half-hidden by a cloud besides, I could see parachutes outlined against the night sky — one, two, at least three.

Then we heard the first shot.

I shrugged and fired my rifle into the woods, up in the trees. One shot, two shots. Leon followed. One shot, two shots. I yelled, "Over there!" and fired again. One shot, two shots. Leon yelled, "Look out!" and fired again. One shot, two shots.

I looked into the sky and didn't see the parachutes anymore. I looked out into the clearing and saw Maurice. He was running back toward the cover of the woods, dragging two things behind him, one in each hand.

I kept firing. Leon kept firing. Richard was firing, too. And then Maurice was back in the woods, and he and Richard were each carrying whatever he had dragged from the open field. We were in the truck and moving within minutes — Maurice driving, Richard in the back with whatever it was.

"So, what is it?" I said.

"They're canisters," Maurice said. "They're made of black leather. You saw how big they are — like three feet. Heavy as hell."

"And where did they come from?"

"London, I think."

That was when Leon and I looked at each other and Maurice burst out laughing.

"What's so funny?" Leon said.

"Your faces — especially yours. Don't you get it? The British are supplying the Resistance with weapons, money, radios, all kinds of things. But they only share if you play along, and they don't think we play along quite enough for their liking."

"So we were stealing from the Resistance?" Leon was incredulous. "We were fucking shooting at the Resistance?"

"First of all, you were shooting over their heads," Maurice said. "Second of all, what's stealing? And third of all, fuck them. We need to eat, too. More than them. And I'll be damned if they're going to run this country when this is over."

"So, the German business?" I said.

"Just a little ruse. I don't know if it worked or not. If nothing else, it confused them a little. We didn't need much time, as you could see. And anyway, I think they got two canisters for their trouble."

Maurice had thought of everything. Back at the camp, Richard informed us of our haul. "I'm not sure what some of this stuff is," he said. "But I'm sure of two things: detonators and money. And I'm pretty sure we can use both of those things."

28

I couldn't sleep, but not because of Manon. I was still wired from our sojourn into the woods and the adrenaline seemed unlikely to ebb. So I was sitting outside the cabin while the rest slept inside. I was reading a tract that Maurice had given me, reading by the light of a torch. It was there that Leon joined me.

"Still too wired? I know I am."

"Yeah," Leon said. "Part of me doesn't know how the rest of them can sleep. Part of me doesn't know how I can't sleep with them. I mean, I'm so damn exhausted."

"But that was just so, I don't know, exhilarating," I said. "I don't know how else to put it. I can't settle down. To see a plan come together like that, all the little details. The German bit might have been hokey, but it was brilliant if you really think about it."

Leon didn't answer. I was trying to read his face, half-obscured in the dark. Anger, exhaustion — probably some combination of the two. After a minute, he reached over and grabbed the paper from my hands.

"Who writes this?" The masthead said it was called *Journal Des Volontaires*.

"They're a Resistance group that Maurice says he admires," I said. "They seem to be big thinkers. They get it."

I leaned over and poked my finger at a particular article. "Read this one. Just this part here."

Leon read along. It said:

"You don't inherit your father's honor the way you inherit his government bonds... We are the sons of the heroes of Verdun, but there are no more heroes of Verdun. Some are mixed into the earth for which they died; others walk around our streets behind the standards of the legionaries, wearing berets and displaying all their decorations, seeming to say to anyone looking at them: 'We have gained the right to be cowards.' But the pale face of the France that has not been soiled asks each one of us, 'What about you?' We can only erase dishonor by an overabundance of honor and sacrifice."

Leon exploded. "So they're cowards?"

"It's not that simp—"

"If they don't pick up a rifle and climb a tree and try to pick off every German private who wanders by, these 60-year-old men are cowards?"

"Calm down." Leon was beginning to spin out of control.

"I can't believe you've fallen in love with these people," he said.

"I think you're overstating—"

"I'm not and you know it. Or you should know it. This is craziness and you've completely bought into it."

"I can't do this anymore," I said. Because I couldn't, the never-ending debates. If Leon couldn't see the need to fight at this point, I was never going to be able to show it to him. At the same time, I needed him around me. But I had no idea how to bridge the chasm. As we sat there, it was filled only with silence, and it was killing me. I had known him for decades and the idea of an uncomfortable silence was never an issue for us. But it was tearing me up as we sat there, the quiet gulf. Him, too. I could tell.

"When we re-connected in Lyon, what was I doing?" he said.

"Smuggling Jews."

Leon and I hadn't seen each other for more than two years, me in Lyon and him in Paris. But, as his efforts to smuggle Jews out of Paris and into Spain or Portugal became more difficult, he enlisted my help and used Lyon as a kind of way-station.

"Doing that, in these times, that makes sense to me," Leon said. "Look, I hate these people more than I've ever hated anyone or anything in my life — and it isn't even close. Trying to save my people from these animals, that's what I should be doing — not taking pot-shots at corporals from the woods and getting innocent people killed in reprisals for no reason."

"It's not for no reason. It's a war."

"It's a war that you can't win one pot-shot at a time."

"We have to try."

"And let me ask you something else: have you ever heard Maurice, the almighty Granite, ever mention the Jews? Ever once? He fucking preaches every night — drunk, sober, everything in between. It's been a little while now and we've heard his philosophy on everything. Loves Lenin. Hates de Gaulle. Loves guerrilla tactics. Hates big forces. Loves rifles, not Sten guns. Hates Goebbels more than Hitler. Loves redheads. Hates the idea of two redheads at once. Loves plum brandy. Hates that he can never find any. Every opinion in creation — but never once mentioned the Jews. Right? Never once mentioned the main targets of persecution. Right? Never heard him say the word 'Jews.' Right?"

The truth was, I had not.

"Not once, right?" Leon said.

"Right."

"And you see how empty this all is if you can't even force yourself to remember, at least occasionally—"

"Okay, I get it," I said.

"You don't get it. You did, but you fucking don't anymore. It's like Maurice has you drugged or something. You're his puppet."

"Fuck you, Leon."

"I love you, buddy, but this is wrong. Somebody has to tell you, and I'm the only one who will."

"Fine, you fucking told me. You done?"

I walked off, not waiting for his reply.

29

We had a ration coupon between us, and that got us the first bottle of wine. We were suddenly flush with currency, after our escapade with the parachuted canisters, and that was enough to bribe the bar owner to give us a second bottle, sans ticket. Maurice, Leon and I sat at a table at the little bar that afforded us a view out of the front window of the place. Across the street was an apartment building that had been transformed into a German barracks.

It was late, well past dark, but between the light from the bar that spilled out into the street and the lit-up windows in the building across the way, it was easy to observe all the comings and goings. They seemed to work day hours, these soldiers, and they seemed to be all buttoned up by 8 p.m. From what we had seen before, and what we had been able to find out, there were 18 men who lived in the barracks. At night, there wasn't even a guard out front. They just locked the doors — we actually saw the one soldier doing it, turning a key inside and then shaking the doors to make sure they were secure.

"Nighty-night," Maurice said.

"You sure they're all inside?" I said.

"I counted," he said. "And they have three vehicles, and you can see them all parked on the curb."

"I don't get it," I said. "They only work during the day? What are they here for?"

"It's a show," Maurice said. "It's a presence. They're not trying to scare anybody — it's like they're trying to ingratiate themselves. You've seen the posters, right?"

"In Lyon, but not here."

"I'm sure they're the same."

The posters were of German soldiers lifting happy French children in their arms, or playing with them, or holding their hands as they crossed the street, or taking off their helmets and letting one of the boys try it on. They were the joyful conquerors, the smiling occupiers. And if they spent most of their afternoons trying to round up young men for STO work details, well, don't you see the joy that is work?

Sunny, cheerful, helpful — and we were going to kill them all. That's what Maurice told us as we sat there.

There had never been any trouble in Mansle for the Germans, which was likely why they just locked the doors and went to bed. They didn't push it, didn't fraternize, seemed satisfied with the tone of friendly overseers. The bar owner said that the soldiers never came to his place to drink, instead purchasing fortification that they drank at home. One of the soldiers, making a liquor pickup, told him that they had turned one of the flats into their own private bar. And if there weren't any women, well, as the soldier told him, "That's what weekend passes to Limoges are for."

Petain had come through on a tour about six months earlier, Maurice said. "The whole town came out. He drove through in an open car and they mobbed it. It wasn't respectful reverence for the hero of the Great War — it was a goddamn cheering mob. They wanted to touch him. They worshipped him." The disgust in his voice was plain. He nearly spat the word "worshipped." Then, after pouring another glass, he said — not really to Leon or me, just to himself — "fucking cowards." It was almost a whisper.

No wonder the Germans weren't worried. If there was such a thing as easy duty in an occupied country, this was it — except for the women, which was where everyone here apparently drew the line. At least that's what was said by the bar owner, anyway. The truth was unknowable — because the building across the street undoubtedly had a back door, and it wasn't as if all 18 of the soldiers could get a pass to Limoges every weekend.

Satisfied that the doors were locked, and they were all tucked in, Maurice turned his attention back to the now-empty bottle on our table. He reached into his pocket and peeled off a few more bills and waved them at the bar owner. We were the last customers.

"Okay, but you have to be out in a half-hour — deal?"

"But there's no curfew, right?" I said.

"Not officially — but I just don't want to draw any attention," he said. "It's quiet here. I want to keep it that way."

"And besides, you make a shitload of money from their business — am I right?" Maurice said. "I'm sure those boys can drink. I mean, there's nothing else to do here at night."

"A half-hour," the bar owner said. He left the bottle and walked away.

Maurice poured all around and described a simple plan. It really couldn't be easier, given the relaxed setup. Besides currency and detonators, the canisters from the earlier night also contained what we learned were incendiary explosives and timing devices — which were really just glorified alarm clocks. There also were, helpfully enough, written instructions describing the assembly of the bombs — and in French, no less. Those Brits had thought of everything.

"You've done this before, right?" Maurice said.

"Yes," I said. "Not Leon, but I have. And with the instructions, a child could figure it out."

"The way I see it, we need seven bombs altogether — one for each vehicle and four for the building — one on each side. Maybe front door, back door, and on a windowsill on the other two sides."

"How many men?" Leon said. These were the first words he had spoken in a half-hour.

"I figure eight," Maurice said. "That's about the most we can get in one lorry — and I think one makes the most sense. Alex prepares the bombs ahead of time. We plant them. Then you move from one to the next, setting the timers — you're going to be bearing the greatest risk, Alex. You do your best to synchronize them, and then we sit back and watch the whole thing blow."

It would have been insanely risky, if not for the fact that the security around the building was non-existent. As it was, it was still fairly risky. I mean, what were the odds that all 18 men would be asleep, that someone wouldn't be an insomniac, or just up for a late snack?

That was what was on my mind. Not Leon's, though.

"What about the rest of the people on the street," he said.

"What about them?" Maurice said.

"The buildings are all wood on the whole street. And there's only a tiny alley on either side of the German barracks."

"So?" Maurice said.

"So the whole street will probably go up with the barracks," Leon said. "Don't you even care?"

Maurice wasn't used to being challenged — that much was obvious. He actually stiffened in his chair. He paused before speaking. When he did, his tone was cold, emotionless, clinical.

"You're exaggerating the risk," he said.

"But not your lack of giving a shit," Leon said.

Then they just stared at each other. Well, glared at each other. After an uncomfortable interval, Leon's eyes dropped first. Once they did, Maurice began describing the rest of the logistics. None of it registered with me, though. All I could think about was Leon, eyes down, so tired-looking, so beaten. He might have finished the rest of the bottle by himself while Maurice got more and more excited about the plan as he described it. I'm not sure I heard any of it, but I couldn't help but notice that Maurice never even seemed to stop to take a breath.

ix minutes.

The first three bombs would go into the lorries, which were parked pretty much end to end in front of the barracks. There were seven bombs altogether, all wired and ready to go. There was no need for camouflage or any other niceties, so each of them was held together by nothing but tape. There was all kinds of excited talk as we prepared for the drive over to Mansle, but it turned pretty quickly to silence as each of the other seven men was handed their little bundle of destruction. I drove.

We arrived on a quiet back road, as was our custom. There wasn't likely to be a German patrol guarding the main street at either end, but there was no sense risking it, either. Maurice gave me directions as I drove, and we ended up on a private farm road that dumped us at the end into the back of the town. We parked behind the bar.

"All right," Maurice said, the rest of us gathered around. He had already given them their assignments for where they should place their bombs. He would be placing his in the first German vehicle. Leon's assignment was the third vehicle, and then around they went — front door, side window, back door, other side window. That part had been settled. What Maurice was doing was pointing them to vantage points where each of them would go after depositing their cargo. They all trotted off a little uneasily, bombs held in two hands, rifles slung over their shoulders. But they didn't have to worry, even if they dropped their precious cargo. Without setting the timers, the bombs wouldn't blow.

I watched them all run away as I crouched in the alley next to the bar. I counted to 30 and then I ran out, too. As I ran, I could see that Maurice and Leon both remained in their places, which wasn't supposed to be the plan. The rest, I could see, had deposited their bombs and were scurrying off to their hiding places.

At the first lorry, Maurice said, "You've got this, right?"

"Now you ask me?"

Maurice half-laughed. Then he said, "No, really."

"Really," I said. "Get the fuck out of here."

He left, and I set the timer. They were pretty precise. You could set them to 30-second intervals. I had planned it out in my head, and had actually run around at the logging camp in an approximation of the task so I was confident. The first timer would be set to six minutes, and then it would go from there. The goal was to have them all blow at the same time.

Five minutes.

The first lorry was set for six minutes, the next for five-and-a-half. The third would be set for five minutes. It really was an easy process — adjust the time, push a button, run. Leon was still there at the third lorry, waiting for me.

"You're supposed to be gone," I said.

"Don't set this one," he said.

"What are you talking about?"

"Just look where we are."

"I don't have time for this."

"Just look," he said.

I looked. The first lorry was at the front door or the barracks, the second a few feet behind the first, the third a few feet farther behind the second. The third was, in fact, not in front of the barracks at all, but in front of the next house.

"Look at this place," Leon said, pointing at the house next door. "It's made of matchsticks. It'll go up in a second — and then the whole block will go up, and you know it. Don't set this one. It's the only chance of saving them."

I didn't have time for this. In my planning, I had given myself only a minute to spare. This was taking seconds. I didn't have seconds. But maybe Leon was right. And maybe, if I listened to him, I could heal a part of the breach between us. I don't know if that's what I figured, or what. But I was starting to feel panicked and just said, "All right, get the fuck out of here."

"Don't set it," Leon said.

"All right. Just go."

I didn't set it.

Two minutes.

The rest of it really was going like clockwork, you should excuse the expression. The bombs were all in place — easy to find, easy to work with. I had to check each one, at least in a cursory fashion, to make sure that none of the wiring had come loose in the jostling of the lorry ride, or the carrying. But they were all intact.

So it was set the clock, push the button, move to the next. Front door: set the clock for four minutes, push the button, move to the next. Side window: set the clock for three minutes, push the button, move to the next. Back door: set the clock for two minutes, push the button, move to the next.

It was all perfect, until I reached the final bomb. As I turned from the back of the house into the alley, I saw that there was a problem: there was a splash of light coming from the window on whose sill the bomb was sitting. As I approached, I could see in the reflection from the mirror above the sink that one of the German soldiers was sitting on the toilet, reading.

I checked my watch. I had about 90 seconds — and that was assuming that the British timers were as accurate as advertised.

My first instinct was just to run — leave the alley from the direction I had entered it and just disappear behind the barracks. But then I thought, what if that gave them an escape route out of the barracks? We had no idea what the inside looked like, and we were only guessing about the damage the bombs would do. You could argue that the other six bombs would be enough. But you also could argue that maybe, just maybe, leaving one side unexploded would make all the difference, that one side not burning would offer safe passage to who knew how many of them. And, well, fuck that.

I looked at my watch again. I had 75 seconds.

I just pressed myself against the wall and waited, peering up at the window over my left shoulder. I was going to have to decide in maybe 30 seconds. Just then, the light spilling into the alley was blocked — I could see, just barely, a soldier in a night-shirt. He stood there, scratched himself, kind of peering into the window of the house across the alley. I don't know what he could see, given that the house was dark, and maybe he couldn't see anything. Because then he walked away and switched off the bathroom light.

I had been counting in my head. I had 45 seconds. So I set the bomb for 30 seconds, pushed the button and ran out of the alley. I got to the street and knew I didn't have time to reach my designated hiding spot. So I just dove beneath the front porch of the house next door to the barracks and covered my ears. I probably made it with 10 seconds to spare.

The explosions didn't go in exact order; British accuracy, my ass. They went first vehicle, front door, second vehicle, back door, opposite side window, and finally the side window where the soldier had just been sitting on the toilet. The third German vehicle did not blow up, but it was moved about 20 feet and pitched over on its side by the explosion next to it. The most dangerous part for me was the flying car parts that peppered the front porch I was hiding beneath and skittered down the sidewalk trailing sparks.

As I crept out from my hiding place, I could hear screaming. The barracks was engulfed in flames, the air hot on my face. The screaming grew louder. The front door opened and two soldiers came out. They were both on fire. The smell of the burning hair and skin was something that would stick with me for a long time. The two of them tumbled down the front steps, then collapsed as they continued to burn. Behind them came two more soldiers. They were not burning. They were staggering, though, one naked, one in a nightshirt, coughing as they emerged from what had become a billowing, acrid cloud.

They, too, fell down the front steps. They were on their knees, choking, gasping. I approached them, trotting. I didn't have a rifle like the others, but I did have a handgun in my pocket. And I stood above the two stricken German soldiers and put a bullet into the back of each of their heads.

PART III

31

The instructions had been to regroup at the lorry within 10 minutes of the explosions. That would give the men stationed behind the barracks a chance to make sure that no one inside was able to escape out the back. It also would give the town an opportunity to focus completely on the fire, clearing the periphery of any curious eyes. Maurice had said, "We won't leave until we have everyone, but don't fiddle around. Ten minutes."

As I made my way back, I headed into the alley next to the bar across the street from the barracks. It was dark, but I could see Leon standing there, his face lit by the glow from the flames across the street.

"Come on," I said.

"No, look."

"I don't need to see it."

"You do need to see it," he said. Then he grabbed me by both shoulders and spun me around to face what we had just done.

Leon had been right. On the one side, the fire had spread to the next two houses, starting with the one whose porch had sheltered me. On the other side — either because of the wind direction or the fact that the third lorry had not exploded — the houses were not burning.

The street was full of people in their bedclothes — men and women, children and grandparents, generations witnessing the conflagration. The benefit of the multiple, cacophonous explosions had been to wake everyone and get them outside — at least, that was my hope. On the sidewalk and in the street, a dozen little dramas were playing out.

At the farthest burning house, a woman screamed as a man ran back inside. The third floor was just starting to go, but the two floors below it had not. The woman's wailing was heart-wrenching — within seconds, the man rushed back out. He was carrying something, and he handed it to the woman, and the screams ebbed into sobs. It was a photo album, and she clutched it to her chest.

On the other side of the barracks where the fire had not yet spread, another woman pointed and cried. She was waving at the roof, beckoning someone to come down. Looking up, it was two someones. Lit by the flames across the narrow alley, you could see a man and a teenage boy standing on the roof, likely father and son. They were holding buckets, undoubtedly filled with water. The woman in the street was crying and waving for them to come down but they were staying, guarding against a stray ember that might float across the alley and onto their roof.

"Let's go," I said, and now it was my turn to grab Leon by the shoulders and turn him into the alley. He didn't react. He just turned back and stared, his face bathed in the orange light. You could feel the heat of the fire, even across the street.

"Come on," I said, and he did begin running then, just as the wail of another woman filled the night. It was when we were running that it hit me: there was no one tending to the dead

Germans out front, no yelling in the German language, no one in his bedclothes carrying a rifle. Eighteen soldiers. Eighteen dead soldiers. Fucking right.

Leon and I were the last two back to the lorry. The other six were ready and waiting, and their adrenaline was overpowering. They were keeping their voices down but there was a non-stop chatter nonetheless, excited, insistent, all back-pats and holy-shits and then some muffled cheers when I got into the front seat with Leon. Maurice was in the driver's seat.

"All set," was all he said. Then he shifted into first gear and we began, up quickly into the hills. At one point, after about five minutes, the road opened up on one side and we all could look down on the little town. I couldn't see if the rest of the houses next to the barracks had caught fire, but the blaze was still lighting the night sky. Like the smell of the burning hair and skin of the German soldiers who had tumbled out the front door, I would never forget the particular shade of orange that painted the dark sky.

Maurice stopped the lorry for a few seconds so we could take it all in. After he restarted, he looked at me and said, "So what happened with the third lorry."

"Didn't explode," I said.

"Why not?"

"Beats me. They're not perfect devices. You saw how they blew up in the wrong order. I don't know."

"That was your lorry, right?" Maurice was looking past me now, addressing Leon. His reply was a silent stare.

We were quiet the rest of the way back to the camp. Intro-spection was not something I was seeking, so I made a point to try to listen to the chatter of the rest of the men in the back of the lorry. I could only hear snatches, but their excitement was still persistent. I had felt the feeling before during a sabotage operation — when the bomb exploded, it was as if everyone involved in the plan had just scored during injury time — and I understood it. Part of me felt it, too — a lot of me. Maybe the difference was that I had seen the neighbors in the street and they hadn't. I honestly felt nothing about the Germans I had shot. It was the neighbors.

We pulled into the camp and Maurice announced, "The last case of Armagnac dies tonight!" The men cheered, and then they told those who had stayed behind all the details. Leon grabbed a bottle and motioned me over to the edge of the woods.

"You going to help me with my piss this time?" I said.

"Yeah, something like that."

"What?"

"I can't take this anymore," he said. "I can't stay."

I had steeled myself for this. And I had told myself for the last few days that I had been ready to have the two of us part when I brought up joining Maurice's group in the first place. I was hoping, deep down somewhere, that he would make the decision to join me, but I honestly believed at the time that it had been a long shot. I was ready.

But since he had agreed to stay with me, well, it made this a harder moment. I had, in just a short time, become used to our new arrangement: me more of the zealot, him more of the skeptic, but together.

"Why?" I said. "Just Maurice?"

"Not just Maurice."

"Then what?"

"It's you," Leon said.

There was a long pause then. He seemed to be searching for the right words. I was searching for my breath, which had been forced out of my body as if I had been gut-punched by one of those Aryan specimens that I had shot on the sidewalk. Finally, Leon ended the silence.

"You set those bombs like the target was some railroad bridge, not a building full of people," he said.

"Full of soldiers," I said.

"And you shot those two Germans like it was nothing. You executed two choking, unarmed, on-their-hands-and-knees soldiers, and you're not even shaking. You haven't even mentioned it. To me, that's a war crime."

"At least you admit it's a war."

"I can't take it," he said. "I can't watch what you've become. And when the reprisals come, I can't—"

"We didn't choose the fight."

"I can't do this," he said. "I can't do it again. I just can't. I'm going to Paris."

"When?"

"Right now." Leon stood up, took a drink, and handed me the bottle. He said, "You remember the name of the bar, right?"

I did. He had told me about the place years earlier. For the first couple of years of the war, it was where I sent him coded letters when I lived in Lyon. The bartender at The White Oak on Rue Suger could always get him a message, he said.

"Take a drink," Leon said, and I did. He reached over and I handed him the bottle. Then he turned and walked down the little dirt logging road, away and into the night. My instinct was to call after him, but I didn't. If he couldn't see that this was a war, a real war, then maybe we both had been kidding ourselves all along.

When I walked back to the cabin, Maurice was inside, in full regaling mode. He had gotten to the point of the story where he was describing the explosions at the barracks, and he thrust both arms upward and yelled, "BOOM!" He yelled it six times, once for each of the bombs that went off, and all six were greeted immediately by a cheer from the circle of men at his feet. With each yell, and each upward thrust, another ounce from the bottle of Armagnac that he was holding in his right hand sprayed into the air.

32

Richard was sent out on a reconnaissance mission the next day. He left at noon. It probably should have been earlier, but the Armagnac made that impossible. Maurice wanted one of the young kids to go with Richard, but he insisted on going alone.

"I can't even consider the roads, even the smallest roads," he said. "This is all back-country, through the woods. Alone is better. You can see that."

Maurice relented. We spent the day nursing our hangovers and waiting for word. The radio was no help — the Germans must have changed their frequencies, and we never stumbled on any of their transmissions. I avoided Maurice until I couldn't. He obviously knew Leon was gone. As he liked to say, it's not like this was a battalion.

"Did he say why?"

"Yeah," I said. Then I waited.

"You going to tell me?"

"No," I said. I waited some more.

"Your friend, your problem," he said. "But he's not going to give us up, is he? I mean, you still trust him?"

"With my life," I said. And I meant it. I meant it more than anything I had ever said. I think Maurice sensed that too, or maybe that's just what I was hoping. Whatever, he just walked away.

Most of the food we had was spoiled, or near-spoiled. What was the difference? Spoiled meat smelled at arm's length. Near-spoiled meat required you to put the filet up to your nose. But either way, the instructions from Maurice were the same: "Just cook the hell out of it." It was the same for the potatoes and vegetables. Everything we ate that evening was cooked to charcoal. But it was all we had, and there was none left at the end of the meal.

Richard returned at about 7, scratched up a bit from his journey through the forests but otherwise unharmed. The first thing he did when he arrived was give Maurice a handbill that he had ripped from a wall in the town.

"It was still wet when I got it," he said. "The German soldier had a bunch of them, along with a bucket and a brush. He was slopping them up on every block of buildings. I followed behind him and it peeled right off."

"Well, that was fast," Maurice said. He read the paper and then passed it to me, and the rest read the headline over my shoulder as I held it:

WANTED FOR THE MURDER OF FOUR BRAVE GERMAN SOLDIERS

WHO WERE DOING THEIR DUTY

AND PROTECTING THE PEOPLE OF MANSLE

The handbill went on to call for anyone with information to report it immediately at a new German barracks on Rue Vert.

"Where's Rue Vert?" I said, seeing out Richard.

"Two blocks from the explosion," he said.

"And what's it look like now?"

"The fire's out," he said. "Everything on the block to the left of the barracks is burned down — about six houses altogether. Everything to the right is fine. It smells terrible all over the town. People are just wandering around — and the people in front of the burned-down houses are just kind of standing there in a daze."

"Soldiers?"

"Everywhere," Richard said. "Going house to house. Walking around with their rifles in their hands, held out in front of them, not slung on their shoulders. Vehicles checking everyone coming in and going out at the end of the main street. The soldiers look pretty shaken up."

"I hope so," Maurice said.

"But how can it only be four brave soldiers?" I said. "There's no way it was only four. There were four on the sidewalk out front. Nobody saw any of the rest leave, right?"

I looked around. Everyone nodded.

"It's propaganda," Maurice said. "They can't admit to 18 dead because it makes them look too weak, too vulnerable. So they admit to the four on the sidewalk who everybody saw, and that's it."

I had avoided reading to the bottom of the handbill because I suspected what was coming. Finally, I forced myself. It was just one sentence, again in all capital letters:

AS A MATTER OF SIMPLE JUSTICE, 10 FRENCH PRISONERS WILL BE EXECUTED FOR EVERY GERMAN LIFE LOST.

"Forty in reprisal," I said to no one in particular.

"It's usually worse," Maurice said.

"It's still not nothing," I said.

"It's still a war, last time I checked," Maurice said. Then he put his arm around Richard and they walked off by themselves for more conversation. The rest wandered away, all except the guy everyone called JP. I didn't know his real name. He was the one who had used Clarisse to deliver the letters to his girlfriend in Limoges.

I asked him, "Where are they even going to find 40 people in Mansle? I mean, that would be about half the town."

"That's not how they do it," JP said. "They pretty much clean out the jails and kill those poor bastards. They'll go through every little town around here and scoop up every wife beater, every armed robber, every vandal, whoever they have locked up. They'll do that, and they'll get the rest from Limoges if they have to."

"And then?"

"And then they just shoot them," he said.

By that point, Maurice was back. He asked JP to leave.

"Richard says they found the unexploded bomb," he said.

"Meaning what?"

"Meaning he was hiding in a doorway across the street when they turned the unexploded vehicle back on its four wheels and found the bomb lying on the street. He said they all ran away when they saw it, and then they waited for someone with a special shield and big gloves to get close to it. Richard said he thought the guy kind of took it apart right there on the street and then brought the pieces over to someone in an officer's uniform."

"So?" I said.

"So, now they know a couple of things. They know what kind of explosive we used. They know what kind of detonator we had. They know that the timer was made in Britain."

"And that it's an imprecise piece of shit."

"Regardless," Maurice said. "They know some things now. It isn't the end of the world — it's not like they didn't know the Brits were supplying the Resistance. I'm sure planes have crashed making deliveries. I'm sure they've come across a lost canister somewhere along the line. But it's sloppy. That's how you give yourself away. We can't be sloppy. You got it?"

I got it. But I still didn't care. At least half of the block, the part to the right of the barracks, was still standing. And if Leon had been there, instead of on the road somewhere between the logging camp and Paris, I would have told him that he had won me over on that part, if nothing else.

But I couldn't tell him what I was thinking, just as I couldn't tell Manon what I was thinking. And so it went, another endless night.

33

We needed to eat. That was the imperative. The berries-on-the-bushes thing was really only an emergency tactic when you were on the run, but Maurice still had the men take turns going on hour-long excursions in the woods to bring back whatever they could find. Besides the berries, there weren't enough squirrels or rabbits in the woods — not that we had the ammunition to waste on them, or the desire to be firing weapons and potentially giving away our hiding place.

We had money, thanks to the canister that fell from the sky, but that was only half of the equation. We needed ration tickets, too. There was a farmer's market every Thursday in Saint-Claud, about 10 miles to the west, and you really needed the coupons to make it work. From what JP said, you could maybe bribe them for an extra cabbage or two, but that was it.

"Everybody knows they're scamming," JP said. "They're supposed to turn over everything they grow, every animal they harvest, but even the Germans know that they don't. They're willing to live with the farmers keeping a little extra for their families, and their friends, and maybe even a little for the black market. But one of the farmers told me the last time, when I tried to bribe him, 'Sorry, brother, but I can't be a pig about this — because the pigs get slaughtered.'"

So they needed ration tickets. But seeing as how they were all away from home, and fugitives besides, it wasn't as if they could present themselves in their hometown city halls for the monthly ration paperwork. It just wasn't worth the risk — because the Germans watched the ration bookkeeping with the sharpest of eyes. It was the best way for them to keep track of people in occupied France because everybody needed the tickets, and everybody needed to provide a current address to obtain them.

Unless, of course, you were willing to forge them or steal them. On this day, our choice was stealing and our town was Saint-Claud. The city hall would likely be sleepy because it was the middle of the month, still almost two weeks before the next coupons were issued and the queue would wind out onto the dusty sidewalk.

"You never know what the reaction is going to be when you try this," JP said. It was for that reason that Maurice always liked to go on these excursions, even though, in the worst case, it was just going to be a little smash-and-grab operation. It wasn't as if these city halls were banks. They didn't have big safes. In general, the ration tickets were locked in a small metal box that, as often as not, was locked in one of the mayor's desk drawers. And the truth was that, even if the mayor or the other town workers were Vichy sympathizers, nobody was going to get themselves killed over a handful of ration cards.

We drove in the back way, as per usual. You wondered how the Germans caught anybody, given the number of unmarked dirt roads. We parked, we walked the two blocks to the city hall, and we went right in the front door. The three of us were armed with pistols but they were all concealed in our coat pockets.

The woman at the front counter sensed there might be an issue almost before the "can-I-help-you" had escaped from her lips. But she was smiling easily, which was a good sign. Her call of, "Mr. Mayor, a minute of your time please," was made without a hint of alarm.

The mayor, overweight and with a cigarette dangling from his lips, arrived at the counter, took one look at the three of us, and said, "Gentlemen," directing us into his office.

"She comes, too," JP said. And so, the clerk walked with us.

We sat down and the mayor pulled out a bottle from a cabinet behind a desk. This was going to be fine.

"I only have three glasses," he said.

"None for me, Mr. Mayor," the clerk said.

"That's fine, then. I'll drink out of the bottle. Not like it's the first time."

So he poured, and we all drank. The mayor took a second long sip then asked, "So what will it be today, gentlemen?"

"Ration tickets," Maurice said.

"The supply is almost exhausted, I think." The mayor looked over at the clerk, questioning with his eyes.

"Not completely exhausted," she said.

"Quickly, then," he said. The clerk looked at Maurice for permission — even having said almost nothing, everyone automatically knew that he was the leader — and he nodded. She got up and left the room. Maurice looked at me and flicked his head toward the door, and I followed her. There was a telephone on the counter, after all. As it turned out, the strong box was kept unlocked and unhidden on a shelf below the front counter. There were ration coupons available for six adult males, one pregnant woman and one young child.

I handed them to Maurice. Pregnant women received a larger monthly ration of most foods, and that was a prize. But Maurice held up the young child's coupons and grinned like, well, like a young child. "Milk," he said. "My God, I can't remember the last time I drank a glass of milk."

"We need to go," JP said, tapping his wristwatch. It was nearly noon and the farmers would be packing up and heading home in a few minutes. Hopefully, they hadn't been picked clean — but Maurice had even thought of that. On the ride down, he said, "It's the time of the month when people are stretching the coupons they have left. They don't have as much to spend as at the beginning of the month. We should be fine."

"Wait a minute — you can't just leave," the mayor said. I didn't get it, but Maurice and JP looked at each other and smiled.

"There's some rope in the storage closet over there," the mayor said. "And hurry."

I quickly realized what was going on. And so, as quickly as we could, we tied the clerk to one chair and the mayor to another chair. This was all for the benefit for the people who eventually discovered them and, more than that, for the Germans.

"How long do you think you'll be here?" I said.

"Oh, less than an hour," the mayor said. "The police chief and I have lunch most days at about 12:30. He's just down the street. I'm supposed to meet him in his office for a sandwich. When I don't show up, he'll come looking."

We were done and getting ready to leave. The mayor said, "Gag us both." And when that was done, he managed to talk through the gag and said, "One more thing."

Maurice stopped him. "Are you sure?" he said.

"Positive."

Maurice sighed. "Not her," he said.

"No, just me."

"Where?"

"The right side of my face," the mayor said. "That's my bad eye, anyway."

Maurice looked at JP, and JP shrugged in return. He looked around and grabbed a heavy book off one of the shelves in the corner. It was the municipal manual, or some such thing, heavy and bound in black leather. JP took one big swing and clocked the mayor on the right side of his face, the binding making solid contact a little below the cheekbone.

The mayor closed his eyes as JP began to swing. The blow toppled him over and he laid on his side, still tied to the chair. The right side of his face was flat on the wood floor, and soon there was blood pooling — but it wasn't gushing out of his mouth. Hopefully nothing was broken except for maybe a tooth — but the evidence would be sufficient for anyone, German or otherwise, who might have any questions.

Maurice and JP made for the door. I leaned over and took one last look at the mayor before we left. Just then, he opened his eyes.

"Vive la France," he said, through the gag that was stained red, the stain only growing.

34

A s it turned out, the farmer's market had been less well-stocked than we had hoped. We did manage to get enough meat and vegetables to feed all of us a decent meal for about three days — or at least what had come to pass for decent — along with some fruit for breakfast. But there was no milk, and Maurice was in a mood for the entire ride back to the logging camp.

The first meal was cooked up as soon as we returned, a veal stew with new potatoes and carrots. We were finished eating by about 3 p.m. and, as was our perpetual state, exhausted. With full stomachs, and without comment, everyone found a place to lie down and nap. Most chose the cabin, but the thought of spending a few more hours in a closed room with a dozen snoring, farting men left me seeking a spot outdoors, beneath a tree.

I found one, maybe 100 feet from the cabin. Richard obviously had the same idea — he was doing what I was doing, sitting and leaning against a tree trunk about 50 feet away. I thought I might be halfway asleep, a minor miracle for me — especially in the middle of the day — but I really wasn't. I was just staring into the green expanse on the far side of the cabin. It was then that I saw it, a quick shiny glint in the afternoon sun. I saw it once, then twice. It was moving, and I attempted to predict its next location, and I did. And in a small gap in the brush, I saw it, probably a button on the uniform of a German soldier. I couldn't see the button, but I did see the soldier, just for a half-second.

My first instinct was to signal Richard somehow, leaning against the tree down the way, but I swallowed it. The last thing I wanted to do was signal what I had seen. The next-to-last thing I wanted to do was stay sitting in the same spot. So I stood up and began unbuttoning my pants as I walked, as if I was headed for a piss. I walked along the trees and sought a spot about 20 feet away, calculating the angles in my head and praying that I was now going to have the cabin in between me and the shiny button I had just seen.

I must have calculated well because there was no gunfire as I made a quick right turn and sprinted for the cabin door. I got inside and went directly to Maurice. He was snoring. I shook him and leaned over and whispered what I had seen, and then he went from man to man, rousing them as quietly as he could.

That's when the firing started. They had Sten guns, and the rotted wood walls of the cabin were exploding as we stood there. Within seconds, there was a six-foot hole in the wall. At least two men were down. The rest, me included, fled out the only door and into the woods. Richard was there already, hiding behind a tree.

"What the—" he said.

"Just run," I said.

And run we did, for probably a half-hour at a trot, not stopping, not looking back, not going near a road, just burying ourselves deeper and deeper in the trees. No one spoke. We simply followed in a line behind Maurice, and we didn't stop until he finally did, in a tiny clearing that was maybe 50 feet on each of its four sides.

As everyone collapsed on the ground, exhausted, I did the quick math. There were still 10 of us. One of the two who were missing was the young kid who had been crying himself to sleep. The other was Ronny, the idealistic one who got drunk with Leon and I after the council meeting in Saint-Junien and brought us to Maurice.

Maurice saw me counting on my fingers.

"They were both dead," he said. "Both got it in the head. I saw that much. Goddamn—"

"I wonder—"

"I don't know," Maurice said. "I don't know."

He looked around and began checking on each of the men. Everyone was supposed to have a knapsack packed at all times, including a pistol and ammunition. Seven of the men had managed to grab theirs on the way out, and the one they called Roger had the biggest prize: the bag containing the radio, the hand-cranked battery recharger, and the remainder of the money. I still had my pistol and Maurice had his. So that left us with nine small guns, the money, the radio, and pretty much nothing else. Food in particular.

"Take the radio," Maurice said. He was looking at me. "Scan around. Try to find a German frequency. Try to find anything. You know how, right?"

"Like riding a bicycle," I said.

"What's Morse code for W?"

"Dot-dash-dash."

"Off you go, then."

"And what if they use a code?"

"Then we're screwed," Maurice said. "But if they're in the field, or in a hurry, sometimes they don't bother."

I cranked the crank for about five minutes, which would give me 15 or 20 minutes of listening time. I put on the headphones, switched on the radio and waited for it to warm up. The dial glowed in the shade of the woods, and then the static began to come through. I twisted the dial slowly, and the static got louder and softer, louder and softer, but I wasn't coming up with anything. Five minutes, 10 minutes, nothing. I was getting ready to quit for a few minutes and begin the recharging process when I heard a transmission through the headphones, faint by definite. And after a few letters, I knew it was definitely in German.

I didn't hear much. I had pretty clearly come upon the end of a transmission. The part I heard lasted maybe three or four minutes, but I was sure about what I did hear. It really was like riding a bicycle. It was, "...two dead. Repeat, two. Identification papers for two more. Eight rifles. Two Sten guns. One lorry. The setup was as we had been told. Full report later. Over and out."

There was that one sentence, and that was the one I couldn't shake. I repeated it over and over to make sure I would remember it exactly. I yanked off the headphones and ran over to Maurice — repeating it, repeating it. And then I told him what I had heard:

The setup was as we had been told.

"You know what that fucking means," I said.

"Calm down, Alex."

"But you can't be—"

"I don't want to jump to any conclusions," Maurice said. "Mostly because I like you. But you have to know who the most likely candidate is."

Leon. God, I hadn't thought of it.

"There's no fu—"

"Like I said, calm down," he said.

"But there's—"

"Stop it — of course there's a chance," Maurice said. "He might have gotten captured, tortured. Or he might have just given us up because he thinks I'm some kind of dangerous animal. The reason doesn't matter."

Leon. My God, Leon.

"But like I said, no jumping to conclusions," he said. "It could be Leon. Or we could have been spotted leaving Mansle after the explosions. Or we could have been spotted leaving Saint-Claud with the food. Let's just relax for a second."

"Relax?" I said. "How can we—"

"We're safe for now. Nobody knows where we are. The 10 of us will stay together for today. Tomorrow, I was leaving for a trip to Limoges anyway — another Resistance meeting. You come with me. I'll ask around when we get there."

When Maurice told the plan to the rest of them, Richard was upset that he wasn't going to Limoges.

"Sweet on that whore?" I said. He just stared through me.

"I need you here," Maurice said. "You keep the money. You can work the radio. Somebody has to be in charge, and you're the only one who can do it."

He put an arm around Richard's shoulders and they walked away, Maurice chopping the air with his free hand as he recited the orders for what to do when he was gone.

35

The meeting in Limoges had been very much like the meeting in Saint-Junien — everyone sitting in a circle, although in chairs this time and not student desks, and everyone offering as little truth about their own operations as was humanly possible while still professing a spirit of cooperation.

My back muscles were tied in a complete knot, mostly because of the lorry in which Maurice and I had been secreted for the drive into Limoges but partly because of the flimsy chair that I was sitting in. I was in the second concentric circle of chairs around the imaginary center. There was a third circle, too — well, a semi-circle behind us — in which the low men from a couple of the groups were sitting.

We were in an abandoned wing of a porcelain factory. There weren't enough men in town anymore to run the place at full capacity — it was a problem for almost every business, and it made for an abundance of available meeting places. But this place meant that everyone would have white porcelain dust on their shoes for the rest of the day.

As they went around the circle, one guy began to recount a

parachute drop of canisters from the Brits that sounded suspiciously like the one that we had crashed without a proper invitation.

"It's important that we continue to change the codes," the guy said, and then he looked over his shoulder at his second, who handed him a sheaf of paper that he distributed around the circle. "The Germans obviously had the old code — either they figured it out or they had a copy all along. Nobody lost one, right?"

He looked from man to man around the circle. He seemed to look at Maurice longer than the rest, but that might have been my imagination. Whatever, everyone shook their head.

"It should have been routine but we could have been killed," he said. "We heard Germans in the woods, and we were under fire. We still managed to get two of the canisters, thank God. Only the uncommon bravery of my men allowed us to accomplish that much. But we were compromised."

Uncommon bravery these days apparently consisted of hiding in the woods while people fired their rifles into the leaves of the trees above your heads, and then waiting until the firing stopped and scooping up whatever was left behind. It was all such bullshit — and if that was the level of truth-telling occurring in the room, it was impossible to calculate what a waste of time this was.

Anyway, there was a lot of head-shaking and mutters of "fucking Gestapo" within the circle in response to the story. In the midst of it, Maurice managed to turn my way and wink. I looked around me to see if any of the other seconds saw him, and I wasn't sure. But he very clearly could not have cared less.

The meeting dragged on, each of them talking about nothing. When the last man was done, from the last Resistance group, one of them — he seemed like a de Gaulle guy, but I didn't really know — stood up and said, "Executive session in five minutes." They all separated, many heading for the bathroom.

"Executive session?" I said.

"That means you're not invited."

"Ohhh, so now it gets serious. Do you have secret hand-shakes and shit?"

Maurice laughed. "No handshakes, just shit. It'll undoubt-edly be a communication from de Gaulle, or some other asshole in London. Follow instructions. Respect leadership. Acknowl-edge our vision. Just another half-hour of my life I'll never get back."

"So where should we meet?"

"Well..." he said. The single word was followed by a mischie-vous smile.

"Ah, you have somewhere to go?"

"I do."

"A red-headed somewhere?"

"Perhaps," he said. "Do you have anywhere to go?"

"I might," I said.

"Is it who I think it is?"

"Perhaps."

"All right, then," Maurice said, again with the dirty grin. "Let's keep this simple, just like every other visit. I'll meet you at 9 a.m. at Place Jourdan, and I'll arrange a very comfortable hiding place in the ass-end of another lorry for us to travel back after that."

As I walked away, I wasn't sure that I was going to see Clarisse. I needed to think on it, and drink on it. I went to Louis' bar, figuring that he still owed me at least a couple. He was actu-ally happy to see me, and I was glad both for the conversation and the fact that I drank for free for about five hours.

Thinking, drinking. One thing was bugging me, and I was glad for the distraction. I summoned it every time my mind drifted to Manon. The thing I couldn't figure out was why Maurice had led no organized mourning for the men we had lost. These were comrades, people we had traveled with, slept with, killed people with. We had all embraced what was supposed to be a greater good as we had embraced each other. Then two were gone, and we were left to mourn alone. Maurice had never acknowledged their loss to the group. All he did was organize more scavenger hunts for berries.

Thinking, drinking — and then I began the walk. It was part stumble, part walk, somewhere between impaired and pathetic. I went past the shopping district, then the cathedral, and then into the warren of narrow streets with half-timbered houses, on and on. I never got lost. Finally, I presented myself at the front steps, pushed open the door, and climbed the five flights of stairs.

36

It is almost like a dream when I look back on it. I was in Clarisse's flat for about 10 hours — three awake, seven asleep. I can only remember one word being spoken the whole time. I knocked on the door, and she opened it and said, "Alex." I didn't reply. I didn't say a thing.

She took my hand and led me into the bathroom. She sat me on the toilet and turned on the taps of the bathtub. I must have looked pathetic, sitting there, head in my hands. I lifted up to look at her, and I guess I was getting ready to say something — I just don't remember. All she did was put her finger to her lips. The teacher was telling me to be quiet, and so I was.

She undressed me slowly as the tub filled — shoes and socks first, then unbuttoning the shirt, then pulling off my undershirt, then the belt and the pants and the rest. She was mothering me. It wasn't sexual, not at all, not at that point.

She stood me up and eased me into the tub. I scrunched down and instinctively dunked my whole head underwater. I was so — I couldn't remember the last time I had bathed in legitimately hot water. Even the baths I had been able to get at Louis' place had been relatively cold affairs. Since then, I hadn't taken a bath at all. Even in my drunken state, I was able to appreciate the luxuriousness of the thing.

Clarisse had a big sponge and some girly-smelling soap — where she found that in 1943 in occupied France was beyond me. She washed me everywhere. I had been close to tears when I arrived, but whatever those feelings were, they melted away in the warm water. And then it was sexual.

I stood and Clarisse dried me, dried me everywhere. Then she led me by the hand to her bed. I laid on my back and watched her undress. I must have been ready to say something again — I have no idea what. All I can remember is Clarisse standing there, naked, with her finger on her lips. And so I was quiet as she lowered herself on me, doing all the work. The next thing I knew was that I was suddenly awakened in her bed, and she was sleeping next to me.

That's when I panicked. I opened my eyes and saw just the tiniest bit of sun creeping between the curtain and the windowsill. Then I felt the hangover — the headache, and the dry mouth, and the vague nausea. When I closed my eyes again, I thought I might still be drunk. And then it all hit me, every bad emotion — but mostly guilt. Crushing, excruciating guilt.

I was physically paralyzed by the effects of the alcohol and emotionally paralyzed by the rest — but I had to get out of there. There were a hundred things I needed to say to Clarisse, but I couldn't summon the courage to say any of them. I didn't need to apologize — she knew my story, and I had done nothing to lead her on. I hadn't done anything but show up drunk and kind of weepy at her doorstep, and she took it from there. I really did not owe her an apology, just an explanation, but I couldn't. The more I thought about it, the more I couldn't manage even a sentence. I hadn't said a word and I still couldn't think of a word to say.

Thanks for the lay but I still love my wife...

The sex was great, but this never happened...

So I bolted. I got out of bed and looked around and couldn't find my clothes. I walked into the living room and saw them there, washed and ironed. She must have done it while I slept. I got dressed as quietly as I could and managed to open the locks without a noisy incident. And then I was gone, carrying my shoes, down the steps and out.

I sat on the front steps of the building and tied my shoes. Then I leaned over and threw up. It was the hangover mostly, but only mostly. I stood up, and I turned and almost went back inside to explain. Or maybe to write a note. Then I thought the note would be even more cowardly than just disappearing. So I turned again and left, the morning still quiet, my head still aching and my conscience not much better.

37

I tried to stand at the bar and drink my first coffee, but I couldn't manage it. So I walked over to a table, with a coffee and a glass of water and my troubles. I nearly missed the chair when I fell into it, making enough noise that the man behind the bar and the two leaning against it turned and looked.

The barman stared long enough that I said, "What, you've never seen a hangover before?" He didn't answer, instead going back to wiping down the dull zinc surface upon which he conducted most of his daily business, the bar scarred over the years and decades by thousands of stray cigarettes, dented by hundreds of slammed glasses. The place where I was originally standing and waiting for my coffee featured a Cross of Lorraine, the Resistance emblem, that had been etched into the surface, likely with a key or a knife. That was the place the barman was wiping down. It was probably just a coincidence. That, or maybe I had drooled a little on the spot.

"Another," I said, holding up my coffee cup. The barman was quick, bringing me not just my coffee and a small glass of water, but a carafe. A peace offering, then. It was appreciated.

I was sitting in the front window, and the sun felt good on my face. Outside, Place Jourdan was quiet. There were just a few people crossing the street, no cars, one bicycle rolling past. It had likely been a bustling spot before the war, the square lined by businesses and restaurants. But, as everywhere in France, it was as if the clock had not only been stopped in the spring of 1940, but turned back.

The clock. I looked over at the bar where a clock ticked loudly. The meeting with Maurice was still about 30 minutes away. Below the clock was a calendar, and I thought: how long since I lost Manon?

Two months. Two months. That's how long I had remained faithful to her memory. Two months.

I forced the thought out of my head, fixating on the statue in the square which was actually a big rectangle. In the center was a large green space, the perimeter shaded by trees, the middle bisected by walking paths in various directions. I thought about gulping down my coffee and water and heading for one of the benches that surrounded the green, but the idea of standing up before it was absolutely necessary kept me in place.

A statue of Marechal Jourdan dominated one segment of the green. It was a tall, classical depiction on a tall stone base. Noble, caped, hand on his sword, preparing to withdraw it from its scabbard and take on some approaching evil — that was the statue. But I knew nothing about him or his career. Right after I had arrived in Limoges, Leon and I had been walking through the square with a local Resistance fighter we had just met, the three of his drunk already and in search of more. I asked the guy — I don't remember his name — about Jourdan, and he said, "He fought during the revolutionary wars."

"With Napoleon?" I said.

"Usually, I think. But if I remember right, not always. And —

again, I'm a little drunk here — but he wasn't some invincible general. If you compared his career to a football game, it was like he won 5-4 on a late penalty."

"And that gets you a statue?"

"Well, that and being a native of Limoges," the guy said. He shrugged. "We don't have much."

The second cup of coffee had raised my metabolism to the point where I was feeling at least sub-human. The hangover would pass — long experience had taught me that. The rest, I just didn't know.

Two months. I thought back to what Leon had once said: "Living through this shit, a month is like a year in regular times." And he was right. There was almost never a moment of relaxation. There was almost never a time when even the most safe and innocent acts were either safe or innocent. There was always a purpose. Every step you took seemed to have a purpose. You never just screwed around. Even getting drunk had a purpose — to forget, or to aid sleep, or both.

But even if I could come to some kind of acceptance of all of that — that Manon really was gone, that two months wasn't really two months, that the idea of fidelity to a memory was stupid, that nothing that had just happened did anything to diminish my love for Manon — there was the other issue. That I couldn't find a way to express those feelings to Clarisse, and that I had just fled with the dawn. Even if I wasn't a shithead the first way, I was definitely a shithead the second way. Then again, if I still couldn't even articulate my feelings to myself, not really, how could I possibly tell Clarisse? And wouldn't she understand that? Didn't it all just speak for itself?

Even though my head was still foggy at best, and the thought of taking a drink actually made me gag, the notion that I would be able to get through this day sober seemed impossible. I didn't have any ration coupons, but I had some money. Maybe I could bribe my new friend behind the bar. I reached into my pocket to see how much I had when I saw Maurice walking across the square. It was a slow amble. He was even turning his head a few degrees to the left so that he could catch the full sun on his face.

I didn't see the lorry pull up. I just heard the squeal of tires as it stopped short. Maurice obviously didn't see it, either, and by the time he heard the sound, it was too late.

Three men piled out — one from the passenger seat and two leaping out of the open bed in the back. The passenger had a rifle. The other two had clubs of some sort. They were on Maurice immediately. The lorry blocked some of what they were doing, but I could tell that Maurice was on the ground. I could see the two clubs taking alternating downward swings. I could see the clubs above the side of the lorry at the apex of those swings, but I couldn't see the nadir. I could only guess.

They weren't German soldiers, but Vichy militia. The Free Guard. I had never actually seen them before, but their uniforms were notorious: blue jackets and pants, brown shirts and floppy blue berets. Within a few seconds, the two with the clubs were lifting Maurice and throwing him into the back of the lorry. I didn't know if he was dead or not — such was the lifelessness of his body as he was tossed around. Only an extra swing of one of the clubs after everyone was back in the lorry told me that Maurice was still alive. I mean, why hit a dead man?

I suddenly noticed the barman. He was standing behind me and holding a tin tray with another coffee. He was watching what I was watching.

"The worst," he said.

"What?"

"The militia. Our French brothers. The fucking worst. The worst of the worst."

He dropped the tray on the table. The cup clattered on the saucer but it didn't spill.

"On the house," he said. He spit on the floor of his own bar and then thought better of it, wiping it with the sole of his shoe.

38

I didn't know what to do, but I couldn't just let them go. I needed to follow the lorry, somehow — but running after it would prove to be equal parts conspicuous and futile.

Then I remember the bicycle leaning against the wall, half behind the bar.

"Your bike?" I said. The barman nodded.

I grabbed whatever bills I had in my pocket and dropped them on the bar. "I need to borrow it. Take this as a deposit."

The barman considered for a second. "Your friend?" he said.

"Yes."

"Keep your money. Keep the bike — I hardly ever ride it anymore, and it's a piece of shit, anyway. But bring it back if you can."

I scooped up half of the money I had dropped on the bar, and just like that, I was outside on the bicycle and on the street. The lorry hadn't been gone for 30 seconds. I could see it about two blocks ahead of me — maybe two-and-a-half, but I could see it. The bicycle wasn't a complete piece of shit, but the front tire was a little low. Even so, I was ignoring the stop signs and making up ground at a decent clip. When I was a little less than a block behind, I settled into an easier rhythm. I was close enough.

Catching my breath, I tried to think. The questions came a lot easier than the answers. How did they know Maurice was someone worth arresting? Could it possibly have been just an unlucky coincidence? Had somebody betrayed him? Could it have been one of the other Resistance groups?

If the questions all seemed to have been dipped in a vat of paranoia, so be it. If you weren't entitled to be paranoid in the French Resistance in 1943, then who was? This just didn't smell right on a bunch of different levels — and the fact that it was the militia doing the arresting, not the Gestapo, added another layer of intrigue.

Like I said, I'd never seen them before. Their reputation was, as the barman's words and his spit suggested, the worst. They were French citizens, working for Vichy, working aggressively against their countrymen. They weren't like the local gendarmes, who were really just working men trying to feed their families. They were caught in a bad spot, and most of them took a pretty relaxed view of their sworn task to arrest members of the Resistance and prevent sabotage attempts. The truth was that probably half of the gendarmes were on our side, actively tipping us off to potential problems. Of the other half, most were willing to turn at least one blind eye where the Resistance was concerned. I almost felt bad for them when they ever did find themselves in a spot where they had to make an arrest. Like I said, they were just trying to make a living in an unlivable situation.

When the Gestapo injected themselves into the situation, it meant the arrival of evil — but at least they were foreigners and at least you could understand their motivation, however depraved it was. The Free Guard was something completely different, evil taken to a higher power.

The story I had heard repeated more than once concerned a militia squad in Nantiat. They'd only been organized for a few months, but I heard this one twice — once from one of the de Gaulle lovers in Limoges, another time from JP when we were still in the farmhouse. Seeing as how the two sources didn't travel in the same circles, I believed it — and it was horrible.

In Nantiat, just outside of Limoges, a farmer and his wife sheltered a four-man Resistance cell in their barn for two nights — hid them, fed them, and then saw them leave at dawn after their second night's sleep. The next day, a militia squad arrived at the farmhouse to question the couple. They put them in separate rooms, the man in the kitchen, his wife in the bedroom.

Regardless, they denied everything. The militia men didn't believe them. They beat the farmer, but he didn't change his story. Then, exasperated, they brought the wife in from the bedroom, grabbed a carving knife out of a wood block, held her left wrist down on the kitchen table and threatened to cut off her finger if the husband didn't tell the truth.

He was near fainting, but the threat on his wife was too much. He admitted that they had hid the Resistance members for two nights. You would have thought the militia men would have been satisfied. But they weren't. Instead of just leaving, they grabbed the wife's left wrist again, slammed it down on the wooden plank table, took the carving knife and hacked off her left pinky and ring finger. Then they took the ring finger, still bearing her wedding ring, and walked across the kitchen to where the husband was tied to a chair. He was barely conscious, but he was still horrified as they held up the bloody ring finger, and the wedding ring, right in front of his face.

And then, as his wife watched and shrieked, they shot the husband in the head. And only then did they leave the farm. That was the Free Guard, in one story. The source was obviously the wife, and even if she embellished, I mean, how much better could it have been? It wasn't as if she could invent the stump of flesh on her left hand.

The militia had local knowledge. They spoke the language. And their reputation was even worse than the Gestapo's when it came to ruthlessness, which seemed impossible. But it was the truth — and now they had Maurice.

The lorry was stopped about a block ahead of me, and I stopped too, getting off the bicycle and pretending to fiddle with the front tire. I could see that Maurice was sitting up in the back, staring in my direction, but there was no way he could have spotted me. I'm not even sure his eyes were open. The driver had gotten out of the lorry and gone into a building — I couldn't see what it was. A minute later, he returned with two bottles. He kept one for himself and tossed one to the men in the back. They immediately opened it — it was just past 9 a.m. but, then again, who was I to talk? — and passed it back and forth. They even poured a little down Maurice's throat. They held the bottle for him, either because they didn't trust him not to use it as a weapon, or didn't trust him not to drink the whole thing down. Or maybe he was too hurt to hold the bottle himself. That was probably it.

In a minute or so, they were moving again. The more I thought about it, the easier it was for me to rule out coincidence. It just didn't make any sense. Maurice had to have been betrayed. The question was, who? As I pedaled along, I kept thinking about that circle of assholes in the porcelain factory, particularly the one whose heroic men had been ducking under the rifle shots Leon and I were lobbing into the canopy of trees. Maybe he knew that Maurice had stolen the canisters intended for his group and was getting even. Maybe they were all getting even. I mean, it wasn't as if Maurice didn't treat them like the crud between his toes — and right to their faces besides.

So maybe it was them, in some combination. Maybe it was

the unnamed redhead — but, then again, if it was her, why didn't they grab him when his pants were around his ankles? Why let him leave and be loose in the city? Or maybe she didn't tell the Free Guard until after Maurice left her place.

Questions. Maybe it was one of the above, or maybe it was the carelessness of always having Place Jourdan at 9 a.m. as the meeting place. I had done it twice, and thinking back on it, Richard had said they had done it at least one other time before that. It seemed innocuous enough, but who knew? Who really knows what gives you away in the end?

After a couple of minutes, the lorry stopped again — this time, for good. They manhandled Maurice out of the back and he was able to walk inside the building, a militia goon holding each arm.

39

The alley next to the building was six feet wide, give or take. Once the Free Guard had gotten Maurice inside, I cruised into the alley and propped the bicycle up against the building. I was just hiding in the shadows, trying to figure out what to do next.

I walked deeper into the alley and saw, at the end, the four-story stone wall of the building had been replaced by a six-foot wooden picket fence. On my toes, I was able to peek over the top and look between the points of two pickets. It was an open dirt area that would have made for a nice little garden — if even an ounce of sunlight ever reached the space. My guess was that the sun was high enough in the sky for a shaft of warming rays to hit the space between about noon and 2 p.m. in July and August. Other than that, the shade was either cool or cold, and persistent most of all. There was no grass growing in the dirt. Three or four tired ferns grew along the base of the wooden fence on the opposite side, and that was it.

I went back to the bicycle, sat on the ground, and tried to think. The only thing I could think to do was try to contact the de Gaulle group for help. The problem was, I had no idea where they had moved. There also was the small chance that they were the ones who had betrayed Maurice — a small chance but not infinitesimal.

My only other two options — seeing as how they were really the only other two people I knew in Limoges — were Louis at the bar where Leon and I had taken those rooms, and Clarisse. The odds that Louis would be able to round up an armed posse for me were zero, I realized. And as for Clarisse, no. Even if she could help — and she might know someone who knew someone else — there was no way. I just couldn't do it.

As I sat there in the alley, someone opened up a window that was about 10 feet off of the ground. If the someone had leaned out and looked down, I was going to be the next one inside. But he didn't.

With the window open, I could hear at least some of what was going on inside. It was mostly chairs or tables scraping along the floor, and the grunting and mild swearing of the people moving the furniture. When it was done, there was a small silence and then a door opening, and some heavy-footed walking, and then a thud. And then someone with a deep and important-sounding voice announced, "Tribunal starts in three minutes. Three minutes."

Tribunal? This was a new one to me. The Gestapo didn't do tribunals — they just fucking shot you. What were the legal niceties all about here? I assumed that the thud was Maurice being dropped into a chair, and that the tribunal was called in his honor. But I really had no idea.

Across the alley — again, it was only six feet — an ancient woman sat in a chair directly opposite the open window. Her window was open, too. She had a front-row seat for whatever was about to happen. Dressed in black, as if in mourning — and who the hell wasn't in mourning, in one way or another? — she had some knitting in her lap, or maybe needlepoint. I couldn't tell — it was all below the sill — but you could sense from the rest of her body movements that her hands were working on something, and that she was paying attention to it. Except she wasn't, not completely.

Because as I looked up at her, she scrunched a little closer to the window and looked down at me. And when our eyes met, she offered me a bit of sign language — her index and middle fingers pointed at her own eyes, and then just her index finger pointed at me. Did I want to watch? I nodded yes. She pointed down and to her right, to a door farther down the alley that provided entrance to her building.

I scuttled along, staying low, and prayed that the door would open quietly. When it did, without even the hint of a squeak of the hinges, I said a silent thank you to the diligence of the concierge. I was up the stairs, two at a time, and to the old lady's door in seconds. She had already unlocked it and left it open. She also had pulled another chair into place, hiding me nicely in the shadows.

The room in the building across the alley was as I had expected. Maurice was seated at a small table, alone. He was barely vertical. Both of his elbows were on the table, and his two hands were holding up his head. Facing him was a longer dining table with three chairs set up on the opposite side. There also was a chair at one end with a tablet of paper and a pencil in front of it. Scattered behind were the rest of the stiff wooden chairs from the dining set, four in all.

Suddenly, the door opened and a half-dozen men in Free Guard uniforms walked into the room — three taking the chairs facing Maurice, the scrivener at the end of the table, and two others who must have been there for the entertainment. The guy at the end of the table stood up and started talking, but I couldn't make out what he was saying. The old lady's perch was great for watching but not so much for hearing, and I needed to hear. With my own sign language — basically just pointing to my ear — I mouthed a silent thank-you and got up to leave. She stopped me for a second and showed me her needlepoint. It was the Cross of Lorraine. I kissed her on both cheeks and sprinted back to the alley.

I had missed the beginning, when they likely read whatever charges they had. That was a big miss for me, because the charges would have given me a hint about how compromised the rest of the group was and how much danger they, and I, were in. I was kicking myself, but there wasn't time for second-guessing. As I got back into place beneath the window, someone was already testifying. My guess was that it was one of the men from the lorry.

"... from one of our intelligence sources that the defendant would be in Limoges for approximately 24 hours, and that he would be in Place Jourdan at 9 a.m. today. That was where my men and I apprehended him. We brought him directly here."

"Thank you. That is all. The prisoner will stand."

There was the scraping sound of more than one chair on the wooden floor. In all likelihood, Maurice was again being supported by a goon on either side.

"Do you deny the charges?"

There was no specific enumeration of what they were. Maurice's response was silence.

"The murders?"

That didn't exactly narrow it down. Maurice's response was still silence.

"The theft?"

Silence.

"The sabotage?"

Silence.

"The treason?"

This was especially rich, a Frenchman accusing a

Frenchman of treason because he fought against German occupiers. Again, Maurice said nothing.

"The treason?" This time, the question was shouted. The accusation boomed and then hung in the air. I would have been able to hear that one from the old lady's flat across the alley. And this time, Maurice did say something in reply. But it was weak, muffled. It sounded like "fuck you," but I wasn't sure. I could only imagine how swollen his face was.

"The prisoner will repeat his statement."

There was another short silence, and then Maurice must have mustered every ounce of energy when he said, "May your god do justice to your evil souls. Vive la France."

Then there was another thud and the sound of a chair skittering along the floor. It was as if Maurice had collapsed backward and missed the chair. I couldn't see him, but I just knew he was laying in a heap on the floor. I couldn't see the rest of them, but I knew the three men were looking down at him from behind the long table, the fourth man had his head down and was busily scribbling what Maurice had just said on his tablet, and the rest of them were sitting there, arms folded, enjoying the entertainment.

40

Into the dramatic silence, a bored-sounding voice intoned, "The tribunal will announce its verdict in five minutes." With that, there was the simultaneous scraping of several chairs on the floor, and a quick thunder of bootsteps, and the gentle slamming of a door. I was surprised they were even going to bother deliberating. Then again, maybe they were just thirsty. In all likelihood, that's what the second bottle was for when the lorry made its stop.

As I sat in the dirt in the alley, I looked down and saw that my hand was shaking. The truth was that if Maurice was known to them, how could the rest of us not be next? I really should be getting on the bicycle and getting out of town. There was nothing I could do here, not realistically. I was scared, and maybe I could alert the rest. How that might help wasn't clear, mostly because I didn't know what the Free Guard knew. But it would be doing something, and it would be creating some distance.

I was just about convinced to leave when I heard some noise from the window above me. The judges, if that's what you called them, were back. It hadn't been five minutes after all. It had been two quick snorts apiece, give or take.

"After deliberating on the matter, the tribunal rules that the prisoner is guilty as charged and will be put to death for his crimes against France."

More chairs scraping. Another thunder of bootsteps. This time, adding to the sounds, was the grunting of the men who undoubtedly were hoisting Maurice off the floor, and the moaning of Maurice.

How much time did I have? Where were they going to kill him? The unalterable truth was that I could not save him — certainly not as long as he was in that building. I was without a weapon and without a clue. I couldn't bluff my way in there and take Maurice out, even if I had a decent bluff — and without a gun, or some assistance, it was folly. It would have been suicide to try.

But if they took him to a prison and held him for a while, there were possibilities — provided that Frenchmen were still running the prison, locals, not the Gestapo or the militia. And if they transported him someplace else to kill him, there were possibilities, too — there was always a chance amid the uncertainty of the streets. So that would have to be my play. I would have to get back on the bicycle and back on the street, a half-block away or so. I would have to wait and watch and hope that some possibility presented itself.

That was what I had decided, until I heard the noise from my left, from deeper in the alley. It was coming from the back garden that never saw the sun. As I crept down closer, the boisterousness grew louder. It sounded like a half-dozen men — laughing, joking. I could smell cigarette smoke.

Then a door opened, and the noise stopped, a bunch of schoolboys suddenly in the presence of the principal. I wanted to peer over the top of the fence but didn't for obvious reasons.

Then I looked around and saw it, a small knothole that was maybe waist high. From my knees, I was able to press my eye up to it and see the panorama before me.

Five men were lined up with rifles. A sixth, the judge who had sat in the middle seat at the table, stood at attention beside them. The door opened again and the same two goons from the lorry dragged Maurice into the courtyard, one beneath each armpit. They propped him up against the wall, but he couldn't stand for more than a second or two. He sank slowly, not falling but sliding down, his back scraping against the stone wall.

He ended up in a kind of fetal position. This seemed to bother the man in charge, who directed the two goons to make another attempt. They grunted as they lifted Maurice, and Maurice moaned, but the same thing happened. The best they could manage was propping him into a seated position against the wall.

"Enough," the boss said. He pulled a handkerchief from the breast pocket of his blue jacket. It was neatly folded and ironed. He must have lived at home, not in a barracks. He held the handkerchief out in his hand, an offering.

"A blindfold?"

Maurice didn't reply.

"Any last words?"

Nothing.

The officer half-shrugged and stuffed the linen back into his pocket, but not before wiping his own mouth. Then he stiffened and gave the order. It was simple and trite and horrifying. It was three words: ready, aim, fire.

Maurice's body jerked against the wall and fell over. The blood was pooling quickly, creating its own terrible mud. Part of me was hoping that Maurice was already pretty much dead as he sat there against the wall, that he was passed out, that he did not hear the final words. But I was kidding myself, and I knew it.

Because I could see, through the knothole, that with the command of "ready," Maurice opened his eyes and stared straight back at the line of rifles that killed him.

And then I ran. My ears were still ringing from the echo of the rifles in the alley. The smell of the gunfire was still in the air. But I was running, and then I was on the bicycle, and then I was pedaling as fast as I could, not thinking, not feeling. The time for mourning would have to be later. But I did stop a few blocks away, just for a quick second. I did it to orient myself, turning until I saw the clock tower of Benedictins station. Then I knew which way to go.

41

I got through the one checkpoint with just a wave, the German soldier unable to raise even an eyebrow at a tired, dirty, middle-aged man on a bicycle in the middle of nowhere. I likely looked too old to be much of a threat — the truth was, most of the Resistance were a bunch of kids. I was too old, too tired, barely making it up even modest hills. I told myself it was because of the piece of shit bicycle with the under-inflated front tire, but I knew. I was beat. I was aging before my time. This war was going to kill me, even if it didn't kill me.

It was somewhere after that when I began crying. It was likely for a bunch of reasons, for my premature aging, for Maurice, for how I had treated Clarisse, for my break with Leon, for Manon. There was a time in my adult life where I went whole decades without crying, but every emotion was just so raw now. There was so much loss, so much death, and there was no end in sight. Not only was there no end, but there was no map and no compass. Forget tomorrow — I didn't know where I was going to be in five minutes. The truth was, I didn't know where I was at that very moment. I was just pedaling in what I thought was the proper direction, hoping to run into something that looked familiar and then navigating from there. But it had been probably an hour since the German checkpoint, and the last hill had been particularly onerous, and I still had not recognized anything. The hopelessness of the whole thing just hit me.

I probably cried for a half-mile, and then I remembered from a couple of months earlier in Lyon when I was in a jam and my mind was racing with recriminations and what-ifs, and I just kept yelling at myself, "Focus, goddammit." It became my mantra, the only thing that got me through the seemingly endless recitation of personal fuck-ups that played in my head. "Focus, goddammit." And here I was again.

At a certain point in the middle of my personal nowhere, a stream ran close to the roadside, and I pulled over for a drink, a splash on my face and a piss. I was pulling myself together when a lorry traveling in the other direction pulled over to the same spot with the probable intention of doing the same. Part of me wanted to ask for directions, part of me didn't want to draw attention to myself — because the truth was, there was a nine in 10 chance that these guys were either Vichy supporters or neutrals who would sell out a stranger in a heartbeat for a little favor with the local Gestapo. Still, I was lost, so I played the pathetically honest card.

"Hey, I'm lost coming from Limoges. Which way is Mansle?" I knew how to orient myself from there, so I figured.

"Mansle. Terrible," one of the guys said.

"My cousins, I know," I said.

"Did they lose their house?"

"Apparently not," I said. "They said they were on the side of the explosion that didn't burn."

"Dumb luck," the other guy said.

"Better than no luck," I said.

The guy told me to continue for about a mile and then take

the left turn at the road "where the big tree has fallen over and broken the fence."

"There used to be a sign there, but the Resistance," he said.

I nodded. The youngest kids in the Resistance made a sport out of knocking down road signs, or pointing them in the opposite direction, all to confuse the Germans. But I couldn't tell if the guy was approving of the whole thing or not, so I just went with the non-committal nod. Back before the Anschluss in Vienna, trying to discern if a new acquaintance was pro-Nazi or ant-Nazi had involved an elaborate conversational dance before you could speak honestly, and this was the same thing, only in French. But then as now, in whatever language, there tended to be a lot of nodding.

Anyway, I got on the bike, found the left turn in question, and was soon enough back at the small clearing that Maurice and I had left a day and a half before. It was late in the afternoon and it appeared that everyone was napping. No one had been left as a lookout. I walked the last hundred yards or so with the bicycle and no one stopped me or even saw me. Maybe it was supposed to have been Richard. He was a couple of hundred feet away from the rest of the group, using his knapsack as a pillow, snoring. The radio and the hand-cranked charger were next to him.

I shook him and he awoke, startled, reaching for a rifle that wasn't there. "Where..." he said.

"Are you sure you had it?"

"No," Richard said. "I guess not. Glad you're back. Where's Maurice?"

I told him. He screamed, "Noooooooo," and stood up and began kicking things and just repeating it over and over. "Noooooooo."

The commotion woke the rest of them, and they came over, and I told them, too. In the space of about five seconds, the disbelief on their faces morphed into anguish and then again into fear. Maurice was their everything. For most of them, Maurice was the reason they had joined the Resistance. He was the smartest among them by a mile — the smartest, the nerviest, the most glib. He was Granite, and he had been everything they could hope for themselves, and now he was gone, picked off at random, picked off as easily as any of them might be. Fear. Yes, that was the look they settled on.

"So what do we do now?" It was JP, and it was more a whisper than it was a question.

"We move in 20 minutes," Richard said. He had stopped kicking things and had wiped his face on his sleeve. "Pack up your bag. Shit if you have to. But 20 minutes."

"Let's think for a second," I said.

"Twenty minutes," Richard said. His voice was just a bit louder the second time. The look he gave me was not hard to decipher. It was not my place. This was Richard's show now. My eyes were locked on his and his were locked on mine when somebody — I never saw who — asked quietly, "Alex, what are you thinking?"

The question clearly infuriated Richard — eyes just tell you so much. Fury, anguish, panic — all of that flickered across Richard's face. And then the same voice asked again, "Alex?" Finally, Richard looked down and our eyes unlocked.

"I just think we need to think about this for a second," I said.

"This demands an immediate response," Richard said.

"It demands a response, but there's no difference between 20 minutes and 24 hours or 48 hours. We're angry. We're in shock. We need that to pass. There's no hurry."

"Our anger will fuel us," Richard said.

"Our anger could get us killed," I said.

With that, we all stood silently. Richard and I were facing each other about eight feet apart, and the rest were arrayed in a semicircle between us. I had no idea how this was going to resolve itself. By all rights, this was Richard's group now. I was the interloper. I had not lived most of what they had lived. I wasn't even French, for God's sake.

Finally, JP broke the silence. He said, "I think we should listen to Alex. I think we should wait."

There was silent nodding among the rest of the group. No one made eye contact, especially not with Richard. After a few more seconds, he stormed off into the woods. He didn't say a word.

42

As it turned out, the only true bit of leadership that Richard had performed in Maurice's and my absence was to send JP into Mansle with the remainder of the cash to buy a half-dozen bottles from the bar across the street from the dearly departed German barracks.

"You must be exhausted, carrying all of that, what, five miles?" I said.

"Probably six," he said. "But when you're doing the Lord's work—"

JP stopped himself short. He welled up.

"What?" I said.

"The Lord's work," he said. "That wasn't exactly Maurice's favorite phrase, but I use it a lot. It's just a habit I can't break. He tried to get me to say 'Lenin's work' instead. It was like a running joke between us."

JP handed me the few francs he had left. I guess I was in charge of the money now. "It took almost every centime," he said. "There's clearly no Resistance discount."

"Discount? There might have been a surcharge," I said. "That guy was interested in only one thing, and that was no trouble. And I'm pretty sure he has it figured out by now that we were the ones who caused all the trouble."

We sat in a circle and started to drink and waited for Richard to slink back from the woods, which he eventually did. While we waited, I mostly just listened to the rest of them reminisce. God, they loved Granite. Every one of them had a story about some instance when he saved them, sometimes physically but more often emotionally. As JP said, "We're all just fucking babies. He knew it and he didn't care. He just grew us up as fast as he could."

"He didn't grow me up — not Uncle Alex," I said. It got a small laugh. "But he opened my eyes. He showed me the purity of our struggle, and that the rest was just bullshit. That's what he told me the first night I got here: 'Fuck the bullshit.' It was a good lesson. Maybe it did grow me up even a little more than I already am."

I raised the bottle I was holding. It was one of three that we had opened and were passing among us. The other two joined me, and we clanked them together. I offered the first of what would be many toasts before the end of the night.

"First toast," I said. "Fuck the bullshit."

When Richard was in place, I veered the conversation toward the previous 48 hours. I told them everything, starting with the Resistance council meeting in the porcelain factory and ending with my ears ringing in the alley. And by everything, I also told them about the redhead, and about getting drunk at Louis's bar next to the chapel, and about how I had spent the night with Clarisse. At that point, I didn't want to hide anything. I figured there was no sense in letting my pride get in the way of telling an accurate story. I couldn't imagine how leaving out the bit about Clarisse would be a problem, but I kept telling myself that I really didn't know what the Free Guard knew about us, and I couldn't have it on my conscience that another man sitting in this circle could die because of my stupid vanity.

"So, all of my cards are now turned over," I said. "Now you all know everything that I know. Any questions?"

Three of them answered at once, all some variation of this: "Who do you think sold him out?"

I went through the possibilities that had run through my own head — the coincidence possibility, or the Resistance sellout possibility, or the redhead possibility, or the careless rendezvous possibility, or I didn't know what. Somebody would build up one of them as a solution, layering on the evidence, and then I would knock it down. We went through all the scenarios that way — build up, knock down. It was an easy game for me, seeing as how I had already been playing the solitaire version for about 10 hours.

Everyone had pretty studiously avoided returning to the subject of our next move. Richard had been silent the whole time since he returned. He looked beaten, and it was clear no one wanted to rub his nose in it. Still, something needed to be said — and I was drunk enough at that point to say it. And if Richard's feelings were hurt, too bad.

"You're all wondering what's next," I said, and everyone perked up a bit. Even Richard sat up a little straighter.

"Well, I'm wondering too," I said. "I have a couple of thoughts, but I'm not going to lie to you — I'm not sure either of them will work. I'm not to the point where I want to share either one of them with you. I need to sleep on it — or not sleep on it, as the case may be. I'm sorry if you think I'm being secretive but it's the only way I know how to operate. I have to be convinced the plan will work before I bring it to you. For me, that's the only way. Then you can pick it apart, but not before." Then I paused.

"Does anybody have a problem giving me 12 hours or so to

think about it?" I looked around, made eye contact with every-body, including Richard. No one said anything.

"Okay," I said. I held up the bottle and looked through the dark green glass, aided by the moonlight. "There are about two drinks left in this one."

"Two?" JP said. He was smiling.

"Fine, three drinks," I said, laughing. It was easily four. "But I'm still going to take it with me over to the tree line and get started with my thinking. There are three unopened bottles, and you guys still have a lot of stories to tell. It's important for you to do that, and it's important for me to do this. We'll talk tomorrow."

I stood up. "One more thing." They were all looking up at me — sadly, hopefully, hopelessly, I couldn't tell.

"Just know that this is only a pause," I said. "Just know that it's only for a little while. Because I want you to know something, to be sure of it, to never doubt it. I want you to know that we will get our revenge. We cannot bring Maurice back, but we will get our revenge. Know that. Remember that tonight when you close your eyes."

I turned, walked a step, stopped. I held the bottle high.

"Next toast," I said. "To the justice of revenge."

43

W e were parked a full block away from the building where Maurice had been executed. I was worried that it was too far away for me to be able to make a proper identification, but to park any closer was too dangerous. Given how few cars there were on the streets anymore, even a block away seemed too close sometimes. We were the only car parked on the block.

The car belonged to Martin, our old friend the vice-mayor of Couzeix. My life had turned upside down about three different times since Martin had driven Leon and I out to that Resistance council meeting in the schoolhouse in Saint-Junien. Leon was gone. Maurice was dead. Clarisse had entered my life, whatever that meant. But when I counted it out on my fingers, I'm not sure it had been even five weeks.

We had been parked there for six hours. I could never leave the car because I was the only one who knew what I was looking for, but Martin and JP could take turns. In fact, our cover story — meager as it was — required that one of them be gone at all times. The story was that we were waiting for another worker to go on a vice-mayor's mission to pick up a Resistance printing press — the same story we had used at the checkpoint on the way to Saint-Junien.

Martin could pretty much wander anywhere he wanted, given his pocket full of vice-mayor paperwork — which meant he could stay pretty much in sight of the car as he ambled around the neighborhood. JP, though, didn't need to be drawing any attention to himself. His best move would be to go to a cafe or a bar and settle in with a drink. With that, the remainder of the ration tickets and the few leftover francs were his.

"One drink and then back. Keep it to a half-hour," I said.

"Yes, Mother."

If a gendarme, or the Gestapo, came by and asked what we were waiting for, Martin would pull out his vice-mayor paperwork and say that the third worker — "my wife's lazy fucking brother" — was late. Then JP would show up in a few minutes with alcohol on his breath, and we would be fine. If Martin wasn't in the car when the questioning started, I would say that Martin was out searching for his wife's lazy fucking brother, and Martin would show up five minutes later, empty-handed except for his fancy vice-mayor paperwork, cursing his wife's lazy fucking brother. It would work.

By all rights, I should have brought Richard with me, not JP. The next day, after everyone had drunk themselves to sleep while mourning Maurice, the hangovers were noticeable but Richard's demeanor was something else entirely. He was not hungover. He was borderline comatose, walking around in his own non-alcoholic fog. When I told everyone about the plan I had settled on, he didn't react at all. He was barely blinking. If I'd had a compact mirror, I might have put it below his nostrils, just to see if his breathing created a little fog.

"Was he like this all night?" I grabbed JP off to the side.

"He never said a word."

"No stories? No reminiscences?"

"I'm telling you, not a word," JP said. "I'm not sure he was even drinking."

People mourn in different ways, which is something you learn with age. I had seen stoic in my time — plenty of stoic. I had also seen a woman throw herself on a closed casket, wailing. A lot of people used alcohol as an anesthetic, but I knew one guy who literally drank himself to death after his wife was hit by a car, which left his two kids as orphans. Nothing really surprised me about mourning. And the truth was, Richard had known Maurice longer that any of the rest and was likely to have been hit the hardest of all.

But the more I thought about it, that wasn't it. Because Richard had begun barking orders in the minutes after I brought the word of Maurice's death. He was very much alive at that point, hardly comatose. It was only when people wouldn't follow him that the cocoon descended. This was not mourning. This was embarrassment.

If I were Maurice, maybe I would have nursed Richard back. Maybe that's what great leaders do, leaders like Maurice, men with that innate charisma. But that wasn't me. I didn't have time for Richard's shit. This plan needed to work — this revenge needed to be had — if our group was to stay together. I felt that pretty strongly, and I felt I owed it to them, and the last thing I needed was Richard's moping to jeopardize the operation. So I took JP. That is, I sent JP to Couzeix on the bicycle, and he and Martin drove back to pick me up.

As we were driving into Limoges, Martin peppered me with questions and kept coming back to a single detail. Three different times, he asked some variation of, "But this is really all about a goddamn handkerchief?"

"Are you not listening?" I said.

"I am. We're going to chase a guy because of his hand-kerchief?"

"Forget the handkerchief. It's a small detail."

"But—"

"Forget the fucking handkerchief."

"But—"

Our target was, indeed, the Free Guard officer with the handkerchief, the judge who sat in the middle of the tribunal, the man who said, "ready, aim, fire." In my mind, he was the only revenge target worthy of the effort. They killed our leader, and we needed to kill their leader — and that's what this guy gave every appearance of being.

We had nowhere else to start but the building where Maurice was murdered. It had to be their Limoges headquarters building. I was only guessing — I had no idea about their structure — but I had to assume that the Free Guard did have some kind of hierarchy, and that our man sat above it, and that he must have been leading at least a loose bureaucracy. So the guess was that he was an executive who worked mostly behind a desk, and that he probably worked day hours.

"The handkerchief," I said, trying again. "This is where it comes in. I'm telling you, it was folded and ironed. That didn't happen in a barracks. The rest of them looked like men who lived with men. Their boots were dirty. Their shaves were indifferent. They had some discipline about them, but it was just different. Our guy, though, was clean. And that handkerchief — I'm telling you, he lives at home with a wife."

"But what if you're wrong?" JP said.

"If I'm wrong, I'm wrong," I said. "If he doesn't work behind a desk in that building, we'll change course and try to find him somewhere else. If he doesn't work days, we'll wait all night. If he lives in a barracks and not at home, we'll re-think the plan. But this is where we're going to start."

And after six hours of waiting, at about 6 p.m., the front door of the building opened.

"Finally," I said.

"Him?" Martin said. He had been half-asleep.

"Yeah — get the bicycle out of the trunk. Just lean it against the building." He was opening the passenger door when JP plopped into the back seat, back from his latest trip to the bar.

"Him?" JP said.

"Yep. And look at that." There were three cars in front of the building, and our man got into a Citroen that was painted the color of the Free Guard's blue uniforms.

He was by himself. He drove out into the countryside in a direction with which I was unfamiliar. I had slid over and Martin was driving us, and he seemed to know the roads. I had to keep reminding him to keep some distance, given that we were in the middle of nowhere and any vehicle would likely be noticed.

It wasn't a long drive — 10 miles, give or take, not even a half-hour. The sign at the turnoff said we were heading toward Razes.

"Is that accurate?" I said.

"Yeah, they must have missed that one," Martin said.

But we were not in Razes. We were at some unnamed dot on the map, a lovely little town, but little. When our man made a left turn off the main road, we were left with a dilemma because there would be no way to conceal ourselves on such a quiet side road. We debated whether to make the turn and decided instead just to pull over, inch our way toward the intersection and look to the left. And what we saw, maybe 300 feet down, was the ugly blue Citroen pulling into a driveway, and our man getting out and being greeted with a hug by a woman holding some shears in one hand and a small basket of flowers in the other.

"Handkerchief," I said.

44

Part of me wanted to do it right then, but the cautious side of my personality suddenly awoke. Caution had been my primary instinct for my whole life, until recently, but I could hear it speaking to me again as we sat there. Wait, it said. Watch. Plan. And I had time because Martin said he was in for as long as it took.

"I told my father-in-law about this one," he said. "We were sitting in the office, and he had scrounged a bottle from somewhere, and we were drinking away the afternoon — it was right after JP came and asked me — and I just kind of blurted it out. He was kind of surprised. He said, 'You never tell me. Why now?' And I said, 'Because it's one of our own.'"

"And what did he say?"

"He asked me if I needed help," Martin said.

"And what about your wife?" I said.

"She doesn't know. She doesn't want to know. As long as I can find a way to scrounge another leg of lamb..."

"So, she's all about the slab of meat, huh?"

"Well, it is what she's used to," Martin said. Then he grabbed himself down there.

Wait. Watch. Plan. I didn't want to overdo it because the town was so damn small that any stranger would be conspicuous, but I did need to have a better look at our guy's daily routine. So we watched him for two days. On the Limoges end, parking in different places, we were able to sit and observe him leaving the building each day at 6 p.m. The mornings were harder, though. One of the days, Martin and I pulled the car over in the same intersection and slept. If a gendarme or anyone happened by, our story was that we got here late and were lost and decided to sleep in the car. Martin still had his magic paperwork if it came to that, and the story about collecting a Resistance printing press was still a good one, and that would hold us.

But you could only do that once. For the second day, Martin parked the car back on the main road and pulled up the hood and napped inside. I took the bicycle and pedaled the last mile or so into the town, balancing an empty can on the handlebars. If I needed to explain to anyone, the car overheated, and I was fetching some water.

As on the Limoges end in the evenings, our guy was very much a man of habit and precision. He left his house each morning, right at 8:30. It was like he was a goddamn banker — the kind of banker that actually murdered people, though, instead of just their dreams.

"So what's the plan?" JP said. We were back at the camp, everyone sitting in a circle. It was going to be simple enough. Given what we had to work with, there really wasn't much of a choice. All we had were pistols. We were going to have to shoot the bastard, and we were going to have to do it from close range.

Given the logistics, it made more sense to do it at his home. That wasn't totally to dismiss Limoges, which had its pluses and minuses: more places to hide quickly, but also a much greater chance of being seen and apprehended on the spot. On balance, though, the little town would work better, mostly because the chances of getting caught in the act were pretty much nil. We hadn't seen a gendarme on any of our visits, and it would be awfully bad luck for one of them to turn up on the small, private road that led to our guy's house.

Part of me wanted to handle it myself, but caution demanded some assistance. We needed at least one other gun, and probably two, on the off-chance that a gendarme did happen by the scene. Then there was the matter — and not a small matter — that our target wore a sidearm as part of his uniform, out of the house in the morning, out of the headquarters in Limoges in the evening, into the house at night. To me, that meant four guns total — two to watch our backs for police plus two to do the actual killing at the house. Plus Martin as the driver meant five.

The two people doing the shooting would be me and JP, and there would be no discussion on that. I was a bit agnostic on the other two, though. Everybody wanted to go. Everybody wanted a piece of the revenge mission. Even Richard roused from his piteous coma and at least acted as if he wanted to participate, but I didn't trust him. It probably wasn't fair but fuck it. For all I knew, he would interject himself into the actual killing at the last second as a way of proving that he should have been leading the mission all along. There was no way I could take the chance.

I would have drawn lots if not for Richard. Instead, I ended up choosing the two youngest, Roger and Emil. I made it out like it was going to be physically arduous, which really wasn't true but at least gave me a rationale. If the rest were disappointed, well, there was nothing I could do about it. Somebody was always going to be disappointed unless everybody came — and that was neither prudent nor possible.

We left at midnight. Martin dropped us at the turnoff from the main road. He had two tasks: to knock down the sign pointing to Razes and to get back in the car and take a nap.

"Just don't sleep past 8:30," I said.

"Are you kidding me? I won't sleep a second."

"You say that, but—"

"Not a second," he said.

The rest of us walked into the town. It was a dark night, clouds covering the moon, and we didn't see a soul. As we approached the private road, I hoped I would be able to spot the same hiding places I had identified on my earlier visits. As it turned out, it was easy even in the dark. It was downhill from the town's main road to the target's house, and there was a line of hedgerows on either side of the private road, at least for the first 30 feet or so. At the end of each hedgerow was a granite boulder, maybe three feet high, and then there were small gullies — I guess to catch some of the rainwater that would naturally flow down the hill. A man lying down on his stomach behind the hedgerow and the boulder, in the gully, would be completely concealed from the main road. The issue was whether they would be completely concealed from the vantage point of the subject's house. It would be close, but it seemed okay — with the car in the driveway providing a last bit of cover. Anyway, that's where Emil and Roger went.

As for JP and I, we went directly to the house and hid in the shrubbery that grew between the building and the driveway. We got there, and we listened, and we waited. At about 7:30, the husband and wife woke up. She washed up first and then began banging around the kitchen. We were right below their bedroom and heard him stomp into his boots. The smell of bacon and eggs filled the air — I was so damn hungry, I felt like short-circuiting the plan and taking them both out in the kitchen before swiping their breakfast. After a few minutes, there were more morning sounds: the gentle clanking of plates and cutlery; the scraping of chairs on wood floors; the flush of a toilet; the jangling of what must have been the man strapping on his sidearm; the call of 'Goodbye, honey'; the light slam of the front door; one, two, three, four heavy steps on the wooden porch.

I looked at my watch. It was 8:30.

45

JP and I had been on our haunches for a minute or two, ready, waiting. As we heard the boots on the porch, I put my hand on his shoulder. Wait. Wait. Too quick and he might run — and then we would all be in the shit.

The man from the Free Guard had backed the car into the dirt driveway. The driver's side was facing the house. He came down the steps and walked the 30 feet to the car. He reached out for the door handle and I whispered to JP, "Ready." When he was inside and the door slammed shut, I said, "Now."

We ran to our positions, me on the driver's side, JP on the passenger's side. The car had started by the time we were in place. The man was reaching for the gearshift with his right hand when he saw us.

"What?" he said. It was an oddly calm first word.

"Both hands on the wheel," I said.

"What?" he said again. But he complied. Then JP opened the passenger door, rolled down the window, and shut the door again. The window on my side was already open.

I had rehearsed a bunch of short speeches that I would deliver at that point but ended up rejecting all of them. There was no time for speeches, and there was no real purpose other than my own satisfaction. So instead, I said, "Do you remember Maurice?"

At that, the man's quizzical calm deteriorated immediately into panic. His lower lip was quivering. He was searching for something to say, maybe for a justification. Or maybe he was wondering how I knew. Whatever, the emotion was now engulfing him as he sat in the front seat of his blue Citroen while the engine idled. It was a good car, well-tuned. The motor was very quiet.

I reached into his breast pocket. The handkerchief was there.

"A blindfold?" I said.

By then, he was officially terrified. He was crying. He knew that I knew. He knew that I had seen. I looked down at the sidearm on his hip, just to be sure, and saw he was pissing himself.

"Any last words?"

He babbled something, but he was pleading even more insistently with his eyes. I was locked on those eyes, the terror in them. I didn't want to let go of that feeling, the notion that I had reduced a murderer to such a pathetic state, but there was the plan to consider. This had taken long enough. Even in this sleepy, tiny town, you never knew.

I unlocked from his eyes and looked at JP. We both nodded. And as we had scripted, we each took a step toward the front of the car.

"Ready," I said.

"Aim." Suddenly, the Free Guard leaned on the horn with his left hand and reached for his pistol with the right. The blast from the horn pierced the quiet morning. Whether it hid the sound of what came next, even a little, didn't really matter.

"Fire." I shouted the word above the unexpected din.

At that, we each fired one shot — me from maybe three feet,

JP from about five. JP got him in the chin. I got him directly between the eyes. There was no question that he was dead.

And then we ran — up the street, up the hill, with Roger and Emil now on their feet, up out of the gullies, scanning the area and then following us. The wife was out of the house, summoned by the horn or the shots or both. When I looked back, she was leaning into the driver's side window of the front seat and wailing. Within seconds, we reached the road where Martin was waiting, the engine idling. We piled into the car. There were two bottles of cognac there, one on the front seat, one on the back.

"I figured," Martin said.

If anyone saw us, or was following us, it wasn't obvious. The wife might have seen us running away, but it was 300 feet and she only would have seen us from behind. Besides, she must have been in shock. She likely couldn't have seen Martin's car and, even if she had, it was black. That was hardly memorable, not like the blue Citroen that now held her husband's body, a blue casket, blue with blood-red trim.

The adrenaline was running so high that I couldn't remember a minute of the drive back to our camp — that's how my mind was racing. I went over the details, again and again, and I really thought we were clean. When we arrived, Martin pulled the remainder of a case of cognac from the trunk. When I looked at him in wonder, he shrugged and pulled the magic paperwork from his pocket and kissed it. "I have another case inside for my father-in-law," he said. "A day in full."

After Martin left, we drank, and we laughed, and we celebrated. JP and I must have re-enacted the final scene for the rest of them in a half-dozen renditions, with the ending cheered each time by a punctuating chorus of "BANG, BANG." It felt good. It felt righteous. I had killed before and I had sometimes wondered — but not this time. Not for a second.

It was the next morning — or, really early the next afternoon — when Martin returned. We weren't expecting him. He looked grim as he approached, the noise of the car waking me and some of the others. He said he had been in Limoges, and he was carrying a handbill. It was seeking information in the "dastardly murder" of Philippe Rondeaux, a general in the Free Guard. Philippe Rondeaux. So that was his name. The handbill also said that 100 French citizens would be killed in reprisal if the murderers were not found.

"Well, that was quick," I said.

"A hundred?" JP said.

"That's a lot, but it's not unheard of."

"That's not why I'm here," Martin said.

"Then why are you?"

"A hundred is a lot," he said. "Way more than are in the jails around here. They'll definitely have to go into Limoges and clean out the jails there to get a hundred."

"Well, that's happened before," I said. I really had no stomach for the reprisal debate, not now. I did it with Leon because, well, because it was Leon. But not now. If anyone had deserved to die, it was Philippe Rondeaux. And if the killing of Philippe Rondeaux had not made plain to everyone that we were soldiers in a war against evil, then they were never going to understand. I just didn't have the energy for the conversation anymore.

"I have something else to tell you," Martin said.

He was silent. I was silent.

"It was a routine curfew violation," he said.

"What are you talking about?"

"It was really nothing, just that, just a little late because of a flat tire on her bicycle."

"Again, what are you talking about?" I said.

"It's Clarisse," Martin said. "She's in jail in Limoges."

PART IV

46

The rest could see how upset JP and I were, and as they wandered over, Martin repeated the news at least three more times. When he was finished, JP asked him, "But how do you know all of this?"

"If I'm in Limoges for any reason, I have a Gestapo contact," Martin said. "I'm supposed to check in — it's kind of in exchange for the freedom of movement that the deputy mayor paperwork gives me. It's really nothing — and the truth is, my wife does have a lazy-ass brother who lives in Limoges. I just tell them I'm taking him to our house for dinner and that's that. He asks me to lean on my father-in-law a little harder about arresting the STO kids. It's just a little dance, maybe twice a month."

"But how do you know about Clarisse?"

"I saw her," he said. Then he looked at me. "Well, when you described her the other day, sitting the car, it stuck in my head. They had four or five of them in leg irons, marching them up the hill to the prison — one woman. It really didn't register either way, although I did look at her. And then I was able to read upside down off his clipboard when my Gestapo captain was answering a phone call. 'Clarisse Morean. Curfew violation.

Flat tire. Maison d'arret.' That's the prison down the street from his office."

The unasked question — what were we going to do about it? — hung there like an oppressive humidity. They were looking to me for some kind of answer, but I was dumbstruck. I just walked away.

I mean, I just couldn't believe this was happening again. The guy I needed to talk to was Leon. Somebody needed to understand what I was going through, but there was no way I could confide in any of these guys, not even Martin or JP. I was all they had left. I couldn't go all basket case on them — it wouldn't help me, wouldn't help them, wouldn't help Clarisse.

But, hell. How could this be happening again? Back in Lyon, forced by a whole cavalcade of circumstances, I plotted to kill a Gestapo officer who had been on my tail for years. The plan had been a good one, too, even if my aim with the pistol had been just a hair off. The problem, though, wasn't totally that the Gestapo man had survived the attack — although that was a big part of it. The problem was that I hadn't thought, and Manon hadn't thought — and she was an intelligence agent with much more training than I had — about hiding her someplace before the attack.

Her thought was that she would say I had left her weeks earlier, and that she could brazen her way through it. But the Gestapo had other ideas, and soon she was in jail. And so began the series of events that ended with she and I running from opposite directions to jump into an airplane that would take us to safety in England.

But Manon was dead — I could actually think the words now without retching and didn't feel the need to kid myself by saying "likely dead" or "almost certainly dead." She was dead, I was leading a small group of maquis in the hills outside of Limoges, and another woman I had begun to grow close to was in prison and likely in mortal danger because of something I had done. Another good plan, and a better aim this time, and now someone else I cared about could very well be in a position to pay the price.

"But we're not sure, right?" I had walked back and found the same silence I had left minutes before.

"I'm sure I saw her name on the list," Martin said. "I saw a woman being marched to the jail in leg irons who looked like the woman you described to me. So, yes, I'm sure."

"I don't mean that," I said. "I mean, we're not sure they're going to take her as one of the hundred. They might even be bullshitting about the hundred."

"Maybe," Martin said.

"What else do you know?" There was something about his tone.

"I don't know anything. But I'm just going to tell you something. There have been a lot of reprisals lately. We have one person in our jail. Most of the towns around here are probably the same. They're going to need Limoges. And I'm telling you — I bet there aren't a hundred prisoners in Limoges today. I don't like the odds."

"But she's a woman."

"Doesn't matter," Martin said. "The more important thing is, she's a number. Whoever is in charge of the roundup, he has a boss just like everybody else has a boss — and he has to make his number. If nothing else, the Germans are fixated on making their numbers. And Clarisse Morean is a number."

I walked away again. They were all fond of Clarisse. She was the big sister a lot of them didn't have. But they also knew that she and I had spent the night together before Maurice was abducted. And if I didn't spell out exactly what had happened, they had imaginations. They likely thought it was a lot more than it was — more communication, more commitment, more something. But I couldn't even explain the relationship to myself, no less to them.

We still had a couple of bottles of the cognac, and they were opened soon enough. We all just sat around, stunned. Martin gave us two more bottles from his father-in-law's stash and then left. I decided just to listen, and what I found was that no one — not one of them, not even JP — raised the possibility of trying to rescue Clarisse from the jail. There were tears being shed, but there was no call to action. They had killed before, there had been German reprisals before, and that was just the way it went. There was no way to stop them, so there was no sense fixating on them.

"Casualties of war," Richard said at one point, except he was drunk enough that it took him three tries to get the "casualties" part out of his mouth. And then he just mumbled, "Fucking war."

He got the last part out fine, and it was repeated by a few others in the circle. No one had anything else to say. Until we fell asleep, it seemed as if the only communication was when someone held out a hand, signaling that he wanted to drink from one of the bottles.

47

I didn't sleep.

I had to get her out.

I didn't know how, but I had to try.

When I told them the next morning, the rest of the group was stunned — and then I was stunned that they were stunned. It was as if I had suggested plundering the Reich Chancellery in Berlin. By the looks on their faces, they thought the notion of rescuing Clarisse was some combination of lunacy and idiocy. A couple seemed bewildered. JP looked sad. Richard, though, was angry and didn't hide it.

"I told you he was a bad idea," he said, to the rest of them.

"Richard—" JP said.

"Shut up, JP. This is craziness. We can't have this from our leader. It's soft. It's worse that soft, it's stupid. You all know it."

Suddenly everyone was looking at their shoes. JP had started to speak up for me, but now he was as mute as the rest. Group dynamics had never been my strong suit, but even I could sense how quickly this had turned against me.

"But it's Clarisse," I said. "You all—"

"You're fucking her — that's what this is about," Richard said.

"Every one of you has a relationship with her — every last one of you," I said. I wanted to take a swing at Richard, and it took every bit of self-control that I could muster not to do it. I physically turned away from him and addressed the rest.

"Some of you love her, deep down, love her like a sister, maybe like a mother. Why can't you—"

"It's not what we do," Richard said.

"Why not?"

"Didn't you ever hear Granite say it? And I quote, 'To get sentimental is to get sloppy, and to get sloppy is to get dead.' I heard him say it 10 times if I heard him say it once. You all did, too — right?"

Eyes raised around the circle. Heads nodded — quick nods, barely noticeable nods, sad nods.

"It's only sloppy if you don't plan it," I said.

"Storming a German prison with, what do we have? Seven pistols? Twenty-five bullets? Yeah, right. Some plan."

"Nobody said storming." As I spoke the words, I really had no plan whatsoever. At that point, storming was a possible option, I guess.

"It's suicide," Richard said. He was vibrant again. As the back-and-forth continued, he was countering my arguments before I managed to get them out. He really was a smart guy. Maybe I should have just shut up and allowed him to lead from the beginning. Who knows? We would have gotten revenge on somebody a day or two quicker, and then Clarisse wouldn't have been in jail when the reprisals were organized.

My head felt like it was going to explode, so I just walked away from the argument. A couple of minutes later, JP followed me.

"Look, I—"

"Why does everybody think I'm some kind of traitor all of a sudden?" I said.

"It's not that, not exactly."

"Then what is it?"

"Richard's right," he said. "It's the sentiment."

"But how can you not—"

"Because you can't," JP said. "You just fucking can't. Look, I don't know what your relationship with her is, but you just can't. If you didn't know her, this wouldn't be an issue."

"If we all didn't know her."

"Same thing. Reprisals are part of this. They have been from the beginning. If you believe in what we're doing, then you can't allow the reprisals to be a deterrent — or we'll never get the fuckers out of here."

"But it's—"

"It doesn't matter," JP said. "It can't matter. That's what Maurice preached. 'The cause over the individual.' Look, I didn't buy everything he said, but he was right about that."

The conversation petered out from there. I didn't remember how it ended, but at a certain point, JP just slinked away and rejoined the group. Roger had caught a couple of rabbits in a homemade trap which meant some meat for lunch, and I did join the group for that. But we ate in silence, and I eventually just worked my way back to the edge of the clearing. The weather was starting to turn, and we were going to need to find shelter again pretty soon. Somebody was going to have to organize the scouting out of a new place — an abandoned farm, something — but the group was essentially paralyzed.

Day turned to night. Martin had brought me a knapsack to replace the one I had lost when the logging camp was raided by the Germans. Inside was a warm shirt, a pencil and some paper, a pair of socks and another bottle of cognac from his father-in-law's case, which would be about a half-case by the time the gift was eventually delivered to the old man. A pistol and four bullets completed the kit.

I took out the bottle and the pistol, lay back and used the knapsack as a pillow. Sleeping was not an option, I knew, but it did feel good to close my eyes. My mind kept working, though. A plan had started to take shape in my head, and it wasn't the worst idea I had ever had — by my reckoning, something just on the good side of a long shot. But that was only half of the issue. The other half was scattered around the dying campfire. I sat up and watched: eight men sleeping, snoring, huddling against the uncomfortable chill. They were hugging themselves, scrunched into the fetal position against that chill — not too bad, not yet, but it would be cold soon enough. And then what? And what did I owe them?

I had joined them. I had fought with them. I had embraced their vision, really Maurice's vision. The clarity of it had excited me. The force of his personality had enveloped me. It wasn't the way Leon said — it wasn't like I was chasing a skirt — but I had been smitten, both intellectually and personally. I was too old to be fooled by the whole glory-of-war thing, but I was also too young to just roll over and take whatever from the Germans. What Maurice and this group offered was a way for me to navigate between those two extremes. It was something I needed — and they had served me and I had served them.

But how could they not see? How could they not feel what I was feeling about Clarisse? And even subtracting those feelings, she was one of ours — didn't we owe her at least an attempt to save her? Or was I just hopelessly overwrought, blinded by my emotions and my history?

I looked over again at the snoring and the shivering. They needed to move forward, but I didn't have an answer for them. They needed to get about the business of surviving, of fighting another day, but I didn't feel as if I could lead them and I didn't feel as if I could follow them.

So I wrote a note by the moonlight. I actually wrote two. The first sounded more like a political tract when I read it over, like some kind of manifesto, but it was my pride talking, not me. It was like I was trying to justify what I was doing, even though I didn't completely understand it myself. So I went with something simpler the second time. I threw the crumpled first version into the dying fire and stood there, watching it being consumed. Then I slipped the second letter into JP's back pocket at he slept on his side. He never moved.

JP,

I have to go now. I know you don't agree, but I hope you can understand. Or at least sympathize. I couldn't live with myself if I didn't at least try. It might not make any sense but, for me, this is the Lord's work.

Vive la France.

Alex

And then I walked away, into the night.

48

I watched from the park across the street, from a bench that felt a lot more comfortable than a splintery plank of wood should feel. It had taken me most of the night to walk there. There was a newspaper in a trash barrel next to the bench, or at least a couple of pages of a newspaper — two weeks old, torn in spots, with a photo of Petain on pages 1, 2 and 4. I pretended to read it but mostly just hid behind it, until I saw the mayor shamble up the front steps and unlock the door.

I waited a minute and then followed him inside. It was only 6 a.m., and the woman who had been working behind the front counter on our previous visit had not yet arrived. The door to the mayor's office was open, and I gently rapped on the glass. Head down, reading something, the mayor was startled by the knock. He stared at me for a few seconds without saying anything, and then his face fell. Only a little of the bruising was still apparent.

"Your friend, I heard," he said. "Is it true?"

"How?"

"I hear plenty."

"But—"

"They all gossip about each other," he said. "The Wehrmacht about the Gestapo. The Gestapo about the Free Guard. The Free Guard about the gendarmes. The gendarmes about everybody. I just listen and shrug. It's a talent I have. So is it true?"

I told him that it was. In fact, I told him everything. I needed for him to trust me, and that was true enough, but I also wanted to tell him. He deserved to know. I had just gotten done with the story of the killing itself, with me seeing it all while staring through the knothole in the fence, when he opened his drawer and took out a bottle and two glasses. He poured one glass and then looked at me.

"Okay for you?" he said.

"Okay? I might kiss you."

I told him the rest as we drank — about the revenge killing, about Clarisse, about me leaving the group. He did have a talent. I just kept talking and didn't want to stop. I even told him about the night with Clarisse.

"So you're in love, that's it."

"No," I said. "Not exactly. Really not at all." And then I kept talking, about Manon and what happened in Lyon. It was just pouring out of me. We had finished a second drink when I finally stopped.

"So, do you think I'm crazy?" I said.

"To want to rescue her? No."

"But do you think I'm smart?"

"Different question."

"But—"

"I think it's time for you to tell me why you're here," he said.

So I laid it out for him. I needed the mayor to make me his deputy — or, rather, to fit me up with all the trappings: the travel pass, the rest of the paperwork, the vehicle and a tank of gas. He asked me how I knew about all of this, and I explained about

Martin without identifying him. It wasn't my place to give out his name. As I was telling him, it dawned on me.

"Wait, do you already have a deputy?" I said. "Are you allowed to have more than one?"

"I don't have one," he said. Then he got up and walked over to a small set of drawers in the corner of his office. He groaned when he bent down and retrieved a file from the bottom drawer.

"Never needed a deputy. Didn't have anyone I trusted. Plus, I didn't want somebody driving around searching for kids hiding in caves, anyway. So I just never named one. But the paperwork is all here."

"So what do you think?"

"Let's have one more," he said. He poured us two fingers' worth of whatever it was. The bottle was close to empty. Neither of us said anything for a few minutes. We just sipped. I was determined that the next word would be his, and finally it was. He looked at his watch and said, "Okay, it's 6:20. Let's see if we can do this in 10 minutes."

"What?"

"Here, you need to fill it out, seeing as how you stole the paperwork from the cabinet. Come on, quick."

One by one, I filled out the paperwork — the credential card, the travel pass, the fuel pass, and something else I didn't recognize. When I got to the bottom, though, I stopped.

"You need to sign my name," he said.

"But I don't even know your name," I said.

We both laughed. He pulled out another form from another drawer, handed it to me and said, "Do your best forgery, but quick." And so, on four different forms, I scrawled the signature of Michel Lorain.

While I was signing, he was prying open a different desk drawer with a letter opener.

"Don't you have a key?" I said.

"I do, but you don't." He reached in and pulled out a tray containing several rubber stamps, an ink pad, and another silver thing that punched a raised seal onto the sheets of paper. He stamped each one, and then put the seal on each one, and then examined his handiwork.

"The signatures," he said, pointing at the sheets. "Don't quit your day job. Now come on."

He was on his feet again, back over at the cabinet in the corner, opening another drawer, pulling out a few files and dropping them haphazardly on the floor. Then he knocked over a few things on the top of his desk, then looked back.

"Okay, come on," he said, again.

I followed him out into the front entrance area. It was still empty. He grabbed a set of keys off a peg behind the counter and we went to the front door. He locked it from the inside and then motioned for me to follow him out a back door. There was a small black lorry parked next to a pump. It wasn't much bigger than a car.

"It's all gassed up," he said. "I'll fill you a jerry can and put it in the back. Now what you need to do is walk around the outside to the front door and kick it in."

"What?"

"It's got to look like a robbery. Go. Quick."

So I did. And then I walked inside and then out the back-door. The mayor was closing the tailgate when I got there.

"Now go," he said. "And, really — don't come back."

"But don't you think maybe—"

"No," he said.

"But you don't even know what I was going to say."

"No, I'm not leaving," he said.

"But don't you think—"

"Here's what I think. The first time you came, with the way

you messed up my face, they probably didn't think anything of it. This time will be harder, I know."

"The Gestapo, they're not fans of coincidences," I said.

"I know, I know. And this will be twice. But I think it looks legit. And if you get out of here now, I can show up to the office and see the door broken in and head right down the street to the gendarmes. I think I can sell it. The Gestapo might give me a little shit because the paperwork wasn't locked up securely, but I'm pretty sure I can survive that. I'm not even going to tell them that the deputy mayor paperwork is missing. I'll just say it was ration tickets and the lorry."

"But—"

"Look, I'm not running and I'm not hiding," he said.

"But what if your friend the chief gets you a heads-up that they're coming for you?"

"I'm not running. No. It would dishonor my name. I won't do that."

"But your wife, your children?" I said. "Wouldn't they be better off with their father still alive?"

"But who can guarantee that? And for how long? They're better off with a good name, and that is what I will leave them, no matter what. But all of this would have a much better chance of working if you would stop worrying about me and just get the hell out of here."

Then he tossed me the keys.

49

I had been anxious to try out my new paperwork on the drive into Limoges, but no one stopped me. I knew it was good, though. I patted the folded paper in my pocket and it made me feel, I don't know, bulletproof. Even if it wasn't true, and even if complacency was beyond dangerous, the confidence lift was meaningful. And necessary.

Even with all of that, I was still going to need some help. The way I figured it, I needed one other man. The only place I could think to find one in Limoges was from the de Gaulle Resistance. The problem was that they likely hated me at that point about as much as I hated them. The other problem was that there was still at least a sliver of a chance that they were the ones who set up Maurice to be captured by the Free Guard. I really didn't think it was true but, well, a sliver is still a sliver.

I didn't know where any of my contacts lived anymore — they'd likely moved as often as I had in the previous few weeks. I didn't know where they set up their office, either, of if they even had an office anymore. The only thing I knew was where they drank — two places, actually. One was The Hawk on Avenue Baudin, which was entirely deserted when I got there. The bartender sat forlornly on a stool at the far end of the bar, polishing a couple of glasses that didn't appear to need polishing.

"All I have is watered-down beer," he said. "We haven't had a delivery in two weeks. 'Maybe tomorrow,' they keep saying. But tomorrow doesn't pay my rent."

The Stoneworks on Boulevard Carnot was my second choice. If they weren't there, I didn't know what I was going to do — maybe drive out to find Martin in Couzeix, although that wasn't really fair at that point. He had stuck out his neck farther already than I ever had a right to expect. I couldn't ask him again — although I would if I had to.

The Stoneworks was busier — two old men at a table, three younger guys standing at the bar. The two men were whispering. One of the guys at the bar was drunk and yelling, and his two friends were trying to calm him. As I walked by them, one of the consolers was in the drunk guy's face and saying, "Come on, she's not fucking worth it." And so it went. War, Gestapo, prison, Free Guard, reprisals, didn't matter.

The bar had a back room where the de Gaulle guys drank in private — a back room with a backdoor, just in case. There was always a guard of sorts sitting at a small table outside the door. When I saw him there, I felt as if I was in the right place, especially since I knew the secret code. It was beyond ridiculous, but knowing it was everything. All I had to do was use Lille in a sentence. The reason Lille was the code word was because it was where de Gaulle had been born. Like I said, beyond ridiculous.

And so, I walked up to the guy at the table and said, "I hear Lille has turned into a real shithole."

I was hoping for some outrage, or a laugh, or a smile, or something — but the guy didn't give me the satisfaction. He just nodded, then stood up and reached into his pocket for a key and unlocked the door. Once inside, I heard him lock it behind me.

Three of them were there, sitting around a table, three of them along with a bottle. They looked at me with the same look you have after stepping in a mushy pile of something. They wanted to ignore me but they couldn't. They wanted to keep talking among themselves but they couldn't do that, either. So instead, Louis — the guy I knew the best, the one with the de Gaulle picture in a gold frame — poured me a drink and mustered all the politeness he could.

And then he said, "So what the fuck are you doing here?"

I explained as best I could, leaving out as many details as humanly possible. I didn't confess to being the one who killed Philippe Rondeaux. I didn't admit to having slept with Clarisse. But I said I wanted to try to get her out of the prison, and that I needed help.

"They haven't started yet, have they?" I said.

"What, the reprisals?" Louis said.

"Yeah."

"No, not yet. They have a certain protocol. They usually give it at least 72 hours, on the off-chance they catch the people who did it. They want to seem reasonable. They want the reprisals to be a last resort. You know, 'You gave us no choice, but...'"

"So, when?" I said.

"At least a day," Louis said.

"Wait, is it on the handbill?"

"You're right — somebody's got one, right?" The guy sitting next to him — Jerome, I think — reached into the jacket that was hanging on the chair behind him and produced the same handbill Martin had brought out to the camp. It gave the drop-dead date, so to speak, in red letters at the bottom.

"So you have two days," Louis said. "They'll follow it, too. They're all about accuracy. Precision. As long as their ledgers are neat, that's all that matters."

Two days, then. We debated back and forth whether they

would stick to killing men and not women, but nobody really believed that. The third guy, whose name I didn't know, said the same thing Martin had said: "I don't think it matters. They've just got to make the number."

Then there was the question of whether or not they would find enough prisoners out in the hill towns, but that was dismissed out of hand. "There's no way," the same guy said. "Even Limoges might not get them to a hundred. They might have to go even farther north."

"Shit," I said, more to myself than to them.

"You might get lucky," Louis said. "If they catch the guys who did it, they might just take whoever is handy in the jails out there and call it even. They'd love to get a poster of the guys who did it and slap that on every wall in the area. You wouldn't know, would you—"

I wasn't going to tell them. I was just going to lie, to brazen my way through it. They didn't need to know. As far as I was concerned, it had nothing to do with anything. But as it turned out, I didn't have to lie. Because Louis' question was interrupted by the key turning in the lock. If there had been some kind of commotion outside, we all would have run for the backdoor. If there had been a knock, we would have run, too — because that was the signal for trouble. If the guy sitting at the table outside knocked, it was because the Gestapo was coming calling.

So nobody was scared, but still — you couldn't help it when you heard the key in the lock. What followed, in just an instant, was the collective holding of four men's breath, the door opening, and then recognition.

It was Leon.

50

We hugged for a long time, long enough to make the rest of them uncomfortable. But we really didn't say anything beyond "holy shit" and "oh, man." Until I said, "What happened to Paris?"

"Day after tomorrow," he said. "Thursday night. There's a produce truck with my name on it."

"But I thought—"

"It takes time," Leon said. "I'm particular about the cabbages I hide beneath. They have to be just so."

While he was waiting for the truck, Leon said he had been doing a few odd jobs for the de Gaulle people in exchange for their help with resettling a couple of Jewish families. He had just returned from a courier job, picking up some new identity cards from the Resistance forger du jour and delivering them to a family of three who lived on the other side of the river. They would be on the way to Toulouse in the morning, and then, hopefully, Spain after that.

After a bit, Leon looked at me and flicked his eyes toward the door, and I nodded. He said, "Look, I want to beat the curfew. Alex will stay with me."

"But wait," Louis said. He looked at me. "What did you want when you came here?"

"Curfew," I said. Leon and I both stood up. "I'll let you know when I have a better idea. Truth is, I don't know myself."

We knocked on the door and were let out into the main bar. When we got outside, I said, "Where to?" That's when Leon told me that he was back in one of Louis' rooms above the bar. I must have looked puzzled for a second, mostly because I had been puzzled for a second.

"The other Louis," Leon said.

"Too many fucking Louis's."

We decided to leave the lorry parked — it was only about a 10-minute walk. As it turned out, the other Louis was just as happy to see me as he had been after the Resistance council meeting. His place, like The Hawk, was deserted. He was stacking the tables and chairs outside when we arrived.

"Let me guess — you're waiting for a delivery," I said.

"Goddamn guys. If you don't bribe them, you wait."

"So bribe them."

"Bribes take money, brother," he said.

We went inside and Louis locked the door behind us and drew the curtains. When he pulled a bottle from a back cupboard and began to pour, I spread my arms wide and said, "I love this man. But—"

"But what?"

"I thought you were tapped out."

"Private reserve," he said. "Selling this would be like selling one of my arms."

When it came time to tell Leon what was happening, I worried about talking in front of Louis — not because I didn't trust him but because I didn't want to put him in danger.

"Don't worry about that," he said. "I can play dumb with the best of them. Besides, you're leaving in the morning, right?"

I looked at Leon.

"Right?" Louis said.

"Maybe the morning after," I said, half-mumbling, half-smiling. Louis sighed.

"No later — and I'm serious," he said.

"As a heart attack," I said.

And then I told them. I told them everything. I started with the day of the Resistance council meeting and ended with that very minute. Again, as with my Resistance group, I didn't leave out a detail because I still wasn't smart enough to know what was important. So I told them the whole thing, including me waking up naked with Clarisse, slipping out of the bed in which we had made love, silently putting on the clothes she had washed and ironed while I slept, and leaving without a word. That, and Maurice's abduction and murder, and the killing that I carried out as revenge, and my abandonment of the Resistance group that refused to help me try to bust Clarisse out of prison.

When I was done, Louis offered nothing beyond, "Mother of God." Leon's reaction was the one I needed, though. I wanted approval, but that was likely pushing it. I would settle for understanding, in whatever form. It might just be the unspoken acknowledgement that is the glue of the best long-term relationships — an acknowledgement that he was listening, that he heard me, and that he was willing to continue.

It was what I desperately needed. It arrived when Leon said, quietly and simply, "So what's your plan? Because I know you have one. You wouldn't be you if you didn't have one."

My voice choked up, just for a second, just for the first word or two, when I said, "Well, this is—"

"Wait," Leon said. He looked at Louis. "You don't need to hear this part. You might be good at playing dumb, but let's not push it. You still have that pretty family upstairs. You don't need to know any more. If they come by and start slapping you around, you can tell them pretty much everything Alex just told you and save your ass. But you don't need to know the rest."

Louis thought for a second. He handed me the bottle. "Take the rest upstairs" he said. Then he paused and said, "Morning after tomorrow. Promise me."

"Promise," I said.

Up in the room, Leon switched on the radio and turned it down low, just to create some background noise — not that Louis or his family could hear from upstairs, but he said he just didn't want to take a chance. He happened upon a broadcast by the infamous Philippe Henriot, Vichy's high priest of broadcast bullshit.

"Our Goebbels," Leon called him.

"How can you even—"

"Shhh. It's easier to fight them if you understand them."

Whenever I listened, and I hadn't for months, Henriot hit on two themes: "the terrorists" and "the landing." Of the former, he was speaking about the Resistance — and let's just say that, like the rest of Vichy, he wasn't a fan. And, well, fine. His basic selling point was that every dynamited railroad bridge hurt French citizens more than it hurt the German occupiers, that it resulted in more food shortages and an understandably sterner posture by the Germans. "If not for the terrorists," was how he began half of his sentences. Or at least it seemed that way.

As for "the landing," he was talking about the widespread belief that the Allies were coming to France. When, nobody knew. But sooner rather than later was the hope, and the invasion through Italy — news of which continued to arrive via the BBC — just continued to raise those hopes. And tonight's broadcast was a two-for-one special, "the terrorists" in one sentence, "the landing" in the next, and then back and forth.

"A cruel joke," he called it. "A delusion. And if the landing ever were to occur, the scourge of Bolshevism would follow immediately on its heels."

"I think the Bolshevism part is new," Leon said.

"Who cares?" I said. Then I stopped myself. "Let's not do this."

"Agreed," Leon said. Then, with a big smile that I might have seen when we were two 20-year-olds on the Karntnerstrasse, he said, "So you're not a shithead anymore."

"I'm working on it."

That was when I began to map out what I had planned. He and I had done this more than once over the years. Deep down, Leon was more daring than I was but he also had a journalist's mind. As he used to say, back when he worked on the paper in Vienna, "You know what a journalist is, right? He's the one who points out the broken branch on the Christmas tree."

So he probed at my plan, testing it along its edges. We talked about a couple of aspects, and I explained, and he poked, and I explained again, and he ultimately agreed.

"What are the odds?" I said.

"Maybe 60-40 for the good guys."

"But we need those German uniforms. Do you think those de Gaulle assholes will help us? I mean, not me — but will they help you?"

"Come with me," Leon said. He walked me across the hallway to the bathroom that Louis had scrubbed into habitability in exchange for extra rent money when we first arrived in Limoges. Then, standing on the toilet, he reached up, moved a ceiling panel, reached inside and wrestled a big canvas bag down through the opening. Inside were the two German uniforms we had worn the night we had talked our way into that Vichy youth camp.

51

Leon asked to borrow the lorry because he wanted to drive two of his newly papered Jews to the train station. I slept an extra hour and then walked to the meeting. Leon was already inside when I arrived. In the first 10 minutes we were there, the nicest thing that Leon's forger du jour said was, "You're insane." So I explained it again, slower the second time. But it didn't help.

"It'll never work," the forger said. His name was Raul. What a Raul was doing in Limoges in the middle of the German occupation was beyond me. There were some Spaniards in the maquis, but they didn't own plumbing repair shops in Limoges. Come to think of it, how soldering pipe jibed with the fine work of a forger was also a little beyond me. But, well, whatever.

"Let us worry about if it'll work," I said. After a minute, he offered a what-the-hell shrug, and then a concern.

"I don't know any German."

"We'll take care of that," Leon said.

"Now let's talk price."

At which point, I pulled both of my pocket inside-out in an exaggerated display of our current situation. It wasn't completely true — Louis had given Leon a few francs — but our man Raul didn't need to know that.

"Now, come on," he said.

"There's almost no cost to you, and you know it," Leon said. The truth was that forgers had to charge mostly because of the specialized paper they needed to buy on the black market or steal in order to make fake identification cards. This was different — a little artwork on normal business stock.

"Okay, when?" he said.

"Now," I said.

"Now as in today?"

"Now as in right now."

"You've got to be kidding me."

"Do I look like I'm kidding?"

"There's no way."

"It's only a woman's life," I said. After what he must have deemed to be a face-saving pause, he began to go about his work. He removed a tile from the floor beneath his work table and removed a metal box. Inside, he already had the hardest part done — a stamp of an SS-ish looking logo. He said he had used it on a petrol permit, but that was meant to be a folded, smudged piece of paper.

"This is formal — it won't work," he said. But he did it, trying a couple of different sheets of paper before coming up with one that, even he acknowledged, "wasn't half-bad." Next, he pulled a drawer out of the wall that contained the tiniest printing press anyone could imagine. It was, seriously, not much bigger than a breadbox. He had metal letters lined up in a tray, and he picked them out and put them on a form. "Just 'Place Jourdan, comma, Limoges'? Are you sure?"

That was it. He inserted the paper, manually worked the press, and the words were now below the logo. "Really not bad," Raul said, proud of himself.

Then Leon typed the text of the letter while Raul put the letters back in place and returned the press to the drawer. All that was required was one official-sounding paragraph, followed by an illegible signature.

As Leon was finishing, Raul was putting away the SS logo stamp when he reached into the metal box and produced another stamp. "Someone said they stole it from a German headquarters garbage can," he said. "But I've been afraid to use it. I don't know what it says."

He stamped it on a piece of scrap paper, and I clapped loud enough to startle Leon as he was getting ready to add the illegible signature to the letter. After he did, I stamped it on the red ink pad, and then on the letter, right on top of the signature — a little crooked, a little messy, hopefully with just the right level of word-a-day-ness.

"BE IT SO ORDERED," is what the stamp said.

I folded the letter carefully after the ink dried and put it in my breast pocket. I was really happy, an emotion I hadn't felt in I couldn't remember how long. I was starting to think our chances were north of 60-40.

And then we got to the door, and I looked out the window, and saw Richard standing on the sidewalk maybe 300 feet away, across the street and down to the right.

52

"Oh, shit," I said. "Leon, come look."

Leon came to the door, peered through the glass and said he didn't know what he was supposed to be looking at. "No, to your right," I said, and then he stopped and stared. Richard was peering into a shop window, undoubtedly watching the door of Raul's shop in the reflection. But then he turned and looked directly, just for a second or two, before settling again for the reflection.

"What the—" Leon said.

"I don't know."

"But—"

"I just don't know," I said. "But it goes without saying that I don't like it."

I needed to think. Leon needed to calm down Raul, who suddenly was having kittens. While he gave Raul the shorthand version of Richard's background, a hundred things flew through my mind, a hundred loose ends that I couldn't tie up but that all led me to the same conclusion: that Richard was the traitor, the one who sold out Maurice and got him killed.

I stared out the window, mute with indecision. Leon was way ahead of me. He usually was.

"It's obvious," he said.

"The details aren't obvious."

"Screw the details."

"But I need it to make sense," I said.

And it didn't, not right then. Richard was Maurice's most loyal lieutenant — at least I thought he was. Richard wanted revenge immediately when Maurice was killed — I was the one who insisted that we slow down. I had never considered the possibility that anybody within the group had been the sellout — not seriously, anyway. It just ran so counter to everything they we did together, everything we lived together — and the rest of them for a lot longer than me. Truth be told, at least a little part of me believed it really had been Leon all along.

But, then, there he was.

"How much danger am I in?" Raul said. He had calmed down.

"Not sure," Leon said.

"But some?"

"Probably more than some."

"Oh, man..."

"All right, let's start here," Leon said. "Do you have a place you can go?"

"You mean, like, go and hide?"

"Yes."

"My wife has family in Bordeaux," Raul said. "We can probably get a train in two hours."

"Kids?"

"No, just me and her."

"Okay, so that's settled," Leon said. "Out the backdoor now — there is a backdoor, right? On the train in two hours."

"Can I come back?" This was harder. Leon and I looked at

each other. Neither of us knew how to answer. Richard obviously knew where we were — but who else knew? If we could find that out, we could maybe offer Raul some reassurance.

I didn't know what to say. Finally, Leon said, "Do this. Stay away for a week. Come back to the shop alone. Do it at night. If we think it's safe, we'll shove a note in the mail slot — just one word on a sheet of paper: 'Safe.' If there's no note, I'm sorry."

Raul left immediately. The truth was, I had no idea how we would be able to assure Raul's safety, no less our own. But we needed to do something. I said, "Look, I'm obviously who he's after. So we split up. We don't even know for sure if he's seen you. So I go out the front door and walk to the left. Richard presumably follows me. You go out the back door and wait in the alley and then get behind him — not too close. I walk like I'm headed for the train station. And then, we just..."

"Just what?"

"Just play it by ear," I said. "Could you shoot him if you had to?"

"Life or death, yeah," Leon said. It was clearly not something he said frivolously. The look on his face was grave. Yes, he meant it. I didn't need to ask a second time.

So out the front door I went, out and to the left. I didn't look behind me, didn't stop and tie my shoe and take a quick peek, didn't do any window shopping that might afford a glance. I had to trust Leon at that point. If Richard got within a pistol's realistic range, and if he reached into his pocket, I had to believe that Leon would be ready. At that point, even a wild, stray shot from Leon's gun would certainly distract Richard for a second or two. Even if Leon couldn't kill him, I had to think he could do that much — and the distraction probably would be enough for me to take cover in a storefront, or behind a parked car, or something. Barring that, the second or two of hesitation would give me a chance to run, which would hopefully take me out of pistol range — or at least accurate pistol range.

But how would it end? Leon could simply kill him but that didn't solve our problem, not completely. We owed it to Raul to find out who Richard might have told about the meeting at the shop. And I needed to know exactly what this had been all about.

I decided as I came upon the open green where the Limoges World War I memorial stood, the one that didn't have any names etched into it. I was far enough ahead of Richard that I could reach the bench in front of the sculpture before he saw me sitting there. He would find me there, sitting, with my pistol in my hand. And then it would happen, one way or another.

I was sitting there, waiting, for 10 or 15 seconds when Richard cleared the last building and came into the open. He didn't see me immediately, but then he did. He clearly saw the pistol, too, and his right hand was in his own pocket. But rather than to draw, or to move closer, his first reaction was to retreat. He stopped and looked behind him. He even took a step. But then he saw Leon, and he stopped. And then he walked toward me, slowly, with neither hand in a pocket.

When he got to within about 10 feet, I said, "That's close enough," and Richard stopped obediently. It was almost as if he was seeking instructions, glad for them, comforted by them. He looked like hell, but then, we all did. After 10 or 15 more seconds, Leon joined us. When they looked at each other, there was the barest of acknowledgement.

"Leon, take his gun and go get the lorry and meet us back here," I said. He reached into Richard's pocket, took the pistol and trotted off, back to Raul's shop. Then Richard and I just stared at each other in silence for two or three minutes, him with his hands in his pockets, me with the pistol in my lap. Finally, he gestured at the war memorial.

"Where did you fight?" he said.

"Caporetto."

"My father was at Ypres."

"Did he survive?"

"He did," Richard said. "He had a cough he couldn't shake for the rest of his life. It kept us all awake, every night, every night until I was 20 — that's when it killed him. You know people who live near the train tracks who say they don't even hear the whistles anymore after a while, that they sleep right through them? Not me. I heard that cough every night — just a fit of coughs every hour or so."

We were quiet for another minute or two.

"Opposite sides," Richard said, pointing again at the memorial.

"Still," I said.

53

We drove to the half-abandoned porcelain factory where the Resistance council had met. It seemed to be entirely abandoned. I didn't know how many shifts a week they were down to, but nobody was working when we arrived. We drove the lorry around back and walked through the same hole in the fence that Maurice and I and the rest had used the day before he was murdered, and we didn't see anyone.

We sat in the same chairs as they had used that day. The circle was a small triangle, though, with Leon, Richard and I all about eight feet apart, as close to equilateral as I could manage without a tape measure.

I wanted to unload on Richard but somehow restrained myself. Rather than a long speech, I went for the simplest of questions. I just looked at him and said, "So?"

During the drive over, part of me thought we would have to beat the information out of him, whatever that information was. But his initial look while we were at the war memorial, and then in the car, left me hoping it would be easier than that. So I started with, "So?" I hoped to begin a relatively easy dialogue.

Instead, I opened a floodgate. Richard wouldn't have stopped at all if Leon or I didn't occasionally redirect him.

"It was the day you and I made all of those vegetable deliveries," he said. That was the day Richard and I were separated, taken to different places by the Gestapo. My conversation with the fellows had been a lark. His, apparently, less so. He said about five times things like, "They threatened me," and, "I was so afraid," and, "You have no idea." But if they even laid a black leather glove on him, Richard didn't say.

"So what was the threat?" I said. Richard just dropped his gaze and shook his head. It was the only thing he wouldn't tell us.

"If you want us to understand—" Leon said.

"They threatened me, all right?" Richard was crying then. We dropped it.

"So?" I said, again.

"They wanted Maurice," Richard said. The Gestapo told him to monitor a certain radio frequency every night for instructions, and to transmit information that could lead to the capture or killing of Maurice. He said they almost never sent him a message, other than generic "what do you know?" queries. He said he did his best to put them off.

"Until the barracks," he said. The next day, Richard was the one sent on the reconnaissance mission. He was the one who brought back the handbill, the one who described the half-burned streetscape.

"I didn't tell them then," he said. "I was too afraid to face them. They'd want to know why I didn't tell them in advance — but I didn't know in advance. But on the radio, they demanded to know our location at the logging camp. I gave it to them."

"And got two men killed," I said.

"They were threatening me," Richard said. He was crying even more. Maybe they had a family member of his in their grip.

Maybe he was just a coward. I didn't know at that point, and part of me felt like stopping right there and beating it out of him. But I didn't, and he kept talking.

"When Maurice got away, they were still furious, even more furious, even more demanding on the radio," he said. "And so, when you went to Limoges for the council meeting, I didn't know any of the details but I gave them what I could."

"And what was that?" I said.

"Place Jourdan at 9 a.m.," he said.

So that had been it. Richard's weakness, or treachery, and Maurice's carelessness had been enough. So that explained it.

"But why the Free Guard and not the Gestapo?" I said.

"Ask them," Richard said. "I have no idea."

That didn't make a lot of sense to me, but I'm not sure it was important. The truth was, there was only one more piece of information that truly mattered. That is, how had Richard tracked me to Raul's shop?

"You did that," he said. "When you came back, after Limoges, you told us every move you made while you were there. You mentioned the bar next to the chapel. I knew the chapel, so I took a shot. I waited outside in the shadows. I was in a doorway of an abandoned shop down the street, half-asleep in the dark, when you and Leon showed up last night. I let Leon go when he left in the morning. I waited for you."

"To kill me?"

"I thought that might end it. I thought it might be enough for the Gestapo to..." He searched for the word. "... to release me."

"And they don't know you're here?"

"No," Richard said. "I didn't want to risk it until I had—"

"Until you had me," I said. With that, Richard's head fell, and he just stared at his shoes.

I was ready to kill him at that point — and there was no doubt in my mind that we had to kill him. Not out of revenge, or some sense of justice, but just to protect ourselves and, less self-ishly, to protect Raul. As long as Richard was alive, Raul was in danger. But the fact that Richard had not yet contacted the Gestapo gave us an opportunity to make this clean.

He was pathetic sitting there, head down, silent. He reeked of cowardice, or maybe he had shit himself. But that's what the Germans did, too. They stole a nation's identity and its freedom, killed its youngest and its bravest — but they also robbed so many of the cowards of their ability to live a quiet, cowardly life. They took from everyone.

I was ready to do it, and I was ready to tell Leon. But then, without a word, he stood up and took two steps toward the pathetic figure in the other chair. Richard never picked up his head. He never even lifted his eyes. And in that position, slumped over, staring at the floor, Leon put a bullet in the back of his head.

Richard appeared to die instantly. It was probably a better death than he deserved. His body fell forward out of the chair, forward and on its left side. As the blood pooled around his head, it mixed with the white dust that covered the floor of the porcelain factory. Some of the dust also got in his hair.

I was stunned. I had said, "Oh shit," at the sound of the gunshot, and then stood up and backed up reflexively, knocking down my chair. I watched Richard's body fall, and I breathed in the residual smell of the shot, and then I looked at Leon. I didn't say a word. I hoped that my face said something like, "You didn't have to." But it didn't seem to matter to him either way.

"Life or death," was all he said.

54

There was so much we didn't know. Maybe they had jumped the gun and started the executions early. Maybe Clarisse wasn't even in the jail that was up the street and up the hill from the Gestapo headquarters buildings. But we had to try. It was our only shot.

It was a simple enough play. I would try to bluff her out with my phony paperwork, and off we'd go. If it went bad, I would start shooting and do my best to get out of there alive. The only question was where Leon would be during all of this. My initial thought was that he should be at my side.

"Wouldn't you think protocol would be that two men would accept the prisoner?"

"Maybe," Leon said. "But let's go through it. It's a woman prisoner, unarmed, coming from a jail. She's not a real threat, so maybe the driver stays in the vehicle."

"Yeah, okay, but if the shooting starts—"

"Here's how I see that," he said. "They'll be armed inside, but the people at the front desk are office workers. They push paper. So, armed but not really ready to shoot anybody. If it came to that, you'd have the jump on them."

"But—" I said.

"No, but here's the thing," Leon said. "You have to remember the guard at the outside door of the prison, the one who's going to let you in. If the shooting starts inside, he'll be right through the door and ready to put one between your shoulder blades. He doesn't push paper. He'll be ready. So someone needs to take care of him if it all goes to shit. I think I'm better off outside and taking care of him there."

We debated it back and forth as we were standing in the woods behind the porcelain factory, changing into the German uniforms. Leon had saved everything — helmets, boots, rifles. My uniform wasn't as tight on me as it had been the last time. I had likely lost five more pounds in the weeks since.

I wasn't sure there was a right answer to our dilemma, but I ultimately agreed with Leon. He would stay in the lorry. I would go inside alone.

The first test of the phony paperwork would be with the guard outside the prison's main entrance. If it didn't fool him, we were screwed. As it turned out, he gave it a quick look and then said, "Fine," and in I went. I'm not sure he could have given less of a shit.

The real test would come next. The entrance area was not much, just a couple of chairs facing a counter that had a gate in it. Behind the counter, a sergeant in a German uniform sat behind a desk. I had been hoping the clerical worker would be a Frenchman, mostly because they could give lessons in not giving a shit. But, well, here we were.

"Sergeant," I said, reaching into my breast pocket and handing over the fake orders. He read them over, extended his arms just a bit as he held them at quite a distance. He obviously needed reading glasses and wasn't wearing them, or wasn't willing to admit that he needed them. Good. Very good. The blurrier the better.

"I've never seen this before," he said.

"I'm only the delivery man."

"I have to check." Then he picked up the phone on the counter and dialed a number with two digits.

"Sir, a question at the front desk."

The sergeant listened. He was suddenly just a bit nervous.

"Yes, sir... Yes, sir... It's about a prisoner."

More listening. A little lip quivering.

"Sir, I believe you need to see this."

I did my best to look nonchalant, but I was suddenly fingering the trigger of the rifle. The sergeant put down the phone and said, "Just a minute." I offered what I hoped would be the universal military smirk-shrug that signified, "Goddamn officers." When the sergeant smiled in reply, I believed I had hit the mark.

I had no idea what I would do if this next officer saw through my fakery. I mean, I would shoot him and the guy behind the counter — but then what? I had no clue where Clarisse might be, or how many rifles were waiting through the next door. She might not even be in the prison at all. Other than retrieving the phony paperwork — that was essential, I believed — I didn't know what else there would be for me to do but get out of there and try to come up with another plan.

I was thinking about all of that when the door behind the counter opened and a pissed off captain stormed through. "Well," he said, and the sergeant shakily held out the paperwork. The captain snatched it from his hand and scanned it quickly, and then he looked at me.

"From Place Jourdan? Well, I'm honored."

I wasn't sure how to reply. But given the tone of the question, I went with army smartass.

"My impression is that they walk around believing everyone should be honored, sir, but I never said that."

The captain laughed. My God, might this really work?

"Who signed this?" he said, staring down a little more closely at the scrawl.

"I don't know, sir. I never got past the front desk."

He banged the sharp edge of the paper as he thought about it. The good news was that he didn't seem alarmed by it all. The bad news was that I was one phone call to Place Jourdan away from having to start blasting.

When he said, "All right, sergeant. Bring the prisoner," I had to do everything I could not to break out into a grin. But then, when the captain walked over and picked up the phone on the counter, I had to do everything I could not to aim the rifle at him and tell him to drop it.

He dialed one number, then a second, and then he stopped. I relaxed. It must have been an internal prison call.

"We need another one," the captain barked. He never identified himself or offered a greeting. He listened and then clearly interrupted whoever was speaking on the other end.

"Just a drunk. Anyone."

More listening. Another interruption.

"We promised 20, and we will deliver 20. The new ration tickets just came out yesterday. It should be easy to find somebody passed out in an alley."

More listening. Then, barking.

"A half-hour, no more." And then the captain slammed down the phone. And then, in quick succession, he walked over to the desk, opened one drawer, then another, until he found what he was looking for. It was a stamp and a red ink pad. Bang, bang, and the paper was stamped: APPROVED. Then he picked up a pen and scrawled his name at the bottom.

The sergeant arrived with Clarisse. She looked haggard but okay otherwise. There was no obvious bruising or other injuries. If they had beaten her, they hid it well.

The captain, hands on his hips, said to her, "Such a pity. I was so looking forward to one more chat this afternoon."

He handed me the paperwork, and then the sergeant walked Clarisse through the gate in the counter. It was only when I was putting the handcuffs on her that she realized it was me.

55

W e hadn't really worked out what was next — not with the same level of detail as the bit at the prison. For instance, we hadn't identified the precise alley where I would change my clothes. We just drove about 10 blocks and then Leon pulled into one.

I had removed Clarisse's handcuffs. She squeezed my hand, and Leon's arm, and we drove along without explanation. I was back into my regular clothes in about two minutes. Leon continued to wear the German uniform. Getting back into my side of the lorry, I wore the German greatcoat and the helmet, but just for appearances. They would be off again at the next stop.

"Why don't you come with me?" Leon said. He was headed for a rendezvous with a produce truck that would, within about two days, get him back to Paris.

"It's just supposed to be you," I said.

"We'll squeeze in — they won't turn you away."

"No," Clarisse said. No explanation.

"Then maybe I'll stay," Leon said. "I can always get another ride. It just takes a day or two—"

"No," I said. "You go. You've done enough. You have people who need you."

"But—"

"No," I said. "Go."

We had decided originally that Leon would wear the German uniform as he drove out to his rendezvous, just in case he needed to talk his way out of a roadblock or another jam. The problem was that he didn't have any paperwork to assist him, and we hadn't settled on a story. Talking back and forth, we didn't come up with anything great.

"Just say it's a woman," Clarisse said. "You have a date. No one will question it."

It was perfect. We rode the last few minutes in silence. As we approached the cathedral, Leon said, "Look, no long goodbyes. Just hop out." I pulled off the helmet and the greatcoat as the lorry rolled to a stop. I looked around. There was nobody in sight, but that wouldn't likely be true for long.

"But—"

"Just go," Leon said. "Right now. You know where I'll be. Come when you're ready." He stopped, looked at Clarisse. "Come if you're ready."

As we stepped out, I said, "Wait."

"I'm way ahead of you," Leon said. He held up a small piece of paper containing one word: *SAFE*. "I'll drop it in his mail slot and then go."

Then he was back driving around the neighborhood surrounding the cathedral, and Clarisse and I began walking behind it — through the botanical gardens, down the steps, then the next steps, then the next. In the short walk, I explained most of what had happened in the previous few days, from the handkerchief to *SAFE*. As we walked — and it didn't take five minutes — we passed only one other person, a man passed out on one of the stone benches. He smelled drunk. Yes, it was the day after the new ration tickets came out.

The heavy door that led to the tunnels opened with an easy shove, and the hinges made less noise than the last time. I suspected someone had oiled them and, just inside, I did see a small oil can. Closed and bolted in, Clarisse and I went about the business of trying to map out the future while simultaneously attempting to ignore our recent past.

We talked for over an hour, in a complete circle. I wanted to go to Paris. She wanted to stay. She never tried to talk me out of my desire. I tried incessantly to change her mind, though. It wasn't because I loved her, because I really didn't. In some ways, having her in my life in Paris would add a complication I neither wanted nor needed. But the danger was the part I couldn't shake.

"You know you can't go back to your house, right?" I said. "If they haven't figured it out by now, they will soon — that you never made it to Place Jourdan."

"I can go back and pack a bag."

"Your life in a bag? Is that what you want?"

"I'll get the bag, get the bicycle. I'll be all right."

"A bag and a bike. Great. That's really living."

"It'll be no different in Paris," she said. "All you can see is that, your life is in a bag, too, but in Paris, you'll have Leon. Well, around here, I have others."

We kept going, around and around.

"I could help protect you."

"I don't need your help."

"Paris will have more places to hide."

"More than the hills around here?"

"But what life—"

"We choose our lives," she said. "We encounter circumstances. We make choices. We go on living. If you can't see that, after everything you've been through yourself, you must be blind." She laughed. "Or dumb. You have choices to make, and you've made yours. And I have choices to make, and I've made mine."

"But—"

"But nothing."

Around and around and around. I could see through the little imperfection in the wooden door that it was night. I was starving but, even more than that, I was exhausted. I hadn't slept more than four hours in the previous two days. But as our discussion petered out into silence, I grabbed Clarisse's hand, then I kissed her, and began to unbutton her blouse. She began to say something, but I put a finger up to my lips. It was the reverse of that one night in her flat. She laughed.

We made love in the dark on a bed of our strewn clothes. And then I fell asleep, a coma that was part exhaustion and part satisfaction. I don't know what time it was when I woke up, but I could tell I had slept for a long time. It was light out — I could see the sun through the little nick in the door. It might have been five seconds before I realized that the door, while closed, was no longer bolted, and that I was alone.

56

The White Oak was pretty much as I had imagined it would be — a little bar along one wall, a few booths along another, and a series of tables and banquettes along a third. There was room for a small musical group — maybe a jazz trio — in one corner, with a tiny wooden dance floor in front of it. I could close my eyes and see the place jumping — sweaty, candles on the tables, carnal anticipation in the booths. But then I opened my eyes and saw what it had become: quiet and a little desperate. Even though there were no German rules against it, Max the bartender said he hadn't hired a band in over a year.

"I was barely making a living before the war," he said. "I just can't afford the music now. And without the music, and with the rationing..."

Max swept his arm across the room. There were only eight patrons, including me.

By the time I arrived in Paris, Leon had been making up for lost time. It was almost as if he was a baker, and the women were taking numbers. It was funny — the women seemed to respect the numbers and never jumped the queue or resented anyone else who was also waiting. The only carnal anticipation was in his booth, and the only sweat was in his room upstairs sometime after 10 p.m.

"I don't know," he said, when I asked him if they were wearing him out. "I'm sleeping about 10 hours a day, every day, day after day. I haven't felt this good in a long time. I promised myself a month to myself, just to recharge. You, too. Then we can talk about what might be next."

Most nights, he would be in a booth with whoever, or a couple of whoevers, charming them, eating whatever Max put in front of him. They always brought me a plate, too. I don't know what Leon had told him, about where we had been and what we had done, but no one seemed to resent that both of us were getting a solid meal every day, often with meat. After a couple of weeks of sleeping and eating, I started to feel like a 40-year-old again, not a 70-year-old. Looking in the mirror one morning, I actually thought my face was starting to fill out again, just a little. After a shower and a shave, I looked almost human.

I didn't get out much during the day, and I didn't really mind. I slept late, maybe caught a little afternoon sun in the small backyard behind the bar, maybe walked around the block once or twice. It kind of made me sad, in a way. Because while the sunshine perked me up, and the exercise felt restorative, the quiet of the city was almost unnerving. Paris had always been such a bustling place when I had visited before the war. Now, nobody drove, the cafes were half-empty at best, and people mostly just took their bicycles or the Metro to work and school and then shuttered themselves inside at the end of the day.

So while Leon did his business in his booth, I tended to read a book by myself in mine. Max had a wall full of books, mostly crap. But crap was fine. I looked forward to it every night, along with the one glass of wine that Max allotted. Because while he might be willing to feed me without ration tickets, there was a strict limit on the free alcohol. Business, after all, was still business.

One night, as I was deep into a French translation of an American Western writer named Zane Grey, Max walked over with a bottle in his hand. I thought he had gone soft and was going to top up my glass. Instead, he handed me a letter. "I guess this is you," he said.

The envelope was addressed to "Leon's Best Friend," care of the bar. Max said it had not been delivered by the postman, but by a lorry driver in the city with a delivery from Bordeaux. He said he got it from another driver who had arrived in Bordeaux from Bayonne, down near the Spanish border. Where it came from before that, he had no idea. It likely would not have gotten through the regular post. Almost nothing got through from the south, other than those pre-printed German postcards where real writing was forbidden. They were pretty much fill-in-the-blank: I am sick, your father is dead, whatever.

But this was an actual letter, even if it contained only this:

SAFE

And a signature:

C

ENJOY THIS BOOK? YOU CAN REALLY HELP ME OUT.

The truth is that, as a new author, it is hard to get readers' attention. But if you have read this far, I have yours – and I could use a favor.

Reviews from people who liked this book go a long way toward convincing future readers of its worth. It won't take five minutes of your time, but it would mean a lot to me. Long or short, it doesn't matter.

Thanks!

If you enjoyed this book, please check out my other work. Here's the web address of my Amazon author page:

https://www.amazon.com/author/richardwake

Thanks!

ABOUT THE AUTHOR

Richard Wake is the author of the Alex Kovacs thriller series.
His website can be found at richardwake.com.

Made in the USA
Las Vegas, NV
03 June 2023

72922948R00163